THE ADELPHI PLAYERS

Routledge Harwood Contemporary Theatre Studies

A series of books edited by Franc Chamberlain, University College
Northampton, UK

**Please see the back of this book for other titles in the Contemporary Theatre
Studies series**

THE ADELPHI PLAYERS

THE THEATRE OF PERSONS

Cecil Davies

Introduced and edited
by Peter Billingham
Bath Spa University College,
Bath, UK

London and New York

First published 2002
by Routledge
11 New Fetter Lane, London EC4P 4EE

Simultaneously published in the USA and Canada
by Routledge
29 West 35th Street, New York 10001

Routledge is an imprint of the Taylor & Francis Group

© 2002 Taylor & Francis

Typeset by Scientifik Graphics (Singapore) Pte Ltd
Printed and bound in Great Britain by MPG Books Ltd, Bodmin

British Library Cataloguing in Publication Data
A catalogue record for this book is available from the British Library

Library of Congress Cataloging in Publication Data
A catalogue record for this book has been requested

ISBN 0-415-27026-X

Cover illustration: The Adelphi Guild Theatre production of Cecil Davies'
The Prince of Darkness is a Gentleman, 1950. Photo: John Dodds.

CONTENTS

INTRODUCTION TO THE SERIES

Contemporary Theatre Studies is a book series of special interest to everyone involved in theatre. It consists of monographs on influential figures, studies of movements and ideas in theatre, as well as primary material consisting of theatre-related documents, performing editions of plays in English, and English translations of plays from various vital theatre traditions worldwide.

Franc Chamberlain

EDITOR'S ACKNOWLEDGEMENTS

I am grateful to Cecil Davies for granting me permission to edit and write the introduction to *The Adelphi Players* and for his advice and comments at all stages of preparing the manuscript. My thanks go to the following who have all given invaluable help, support and advice at different times: Wilfred Harrison, who first made me aware of Richard Ward and the Adelphis, and former Adelphis Greta Plowman, Bettina Headley and her late husband, John Headley. We are also very grateful to John Dodds for generously agreeing to the inclusion of his excellent photographs in the book. My former employers, the School of Dance and Theatre at Bretton Hall Colleges were very generous in providing a research sabbatical to help facilitate the completion of this book. In that context, I wish to make special thanks to Tony Green and Paul Cowen and also to thank Linda Taylor, Douglas Hankin, Arthur Pritchard and Wendy Johnston. Additionally, I express my gratitude to Deborah Brooke for her invaluable help in proof-reading at early draft stages. Special thanks are extended to Sally Njampa for her valued contribution in indexing and proof-reading the final manuscript. I would also like to acknowledge the professional expertise and advice of Limelight Photography and Video Production, Charter Square, Sheffield, for their role in helping to prepare archive photographs for reproduction in the book. Finally, I would like to express personal thanks and appreciation to Marilyn for her constant support and enthusiasm for my work.

Peter Billingham

AUTHOR'S ACKNOWLEDGEMENT

I want to to put on record my thanks to Dr Peter Billingham for his work in introducing and editing this volume, thus making it accessible to scholars of the twenty-first century. Without his interest, his specialised knowledge of the small touring companies of that period and his sensitive handling of the task, it would never have seen the light of day. I am particularly grateful to him for his readiness to understand and act upon any suggestions made by me to retain the original, mid-twentieth-century character of the material, vocabulary and style.

Cecil Davies

LIST OF PLATES

INTRODUCTION

In this introduction I wish to place Cecil Davies' unique, first-hand account of the Adelphi Players into a broader historical context whilst simultaneously evaluating the manuscript as a primary source document. It is one which, I believe, is of relevance to anyone – whether scholar, student or enthusiastic layperson – with an interest in the development of touring community theatre in twentieth-century Britain. In placing the manuscript in its proper context I shall inevitably consider the founder of the Players, Richard Heron Ward (1910–69) and his manifesto article "The Theatre of Persons".

Before proceeding to examine Ward's article and ideas in any detail, it is essential to consider the broader social, cultural and ideological background against which Ward's views and aims need to be understood.

In 1938, in a speech delivered in Paris under the title "The Future of English Poetic Drama", W. H. Auden asserted that:

> The dramatist today must show man in relation to nature . . . He must show the reaction in private and public life upon the individual and upon society . . . What will happen to the stage I do not know, but I know this: that the search for a dramatic form is very closely bound up with something much wider and much more important, which is the search for a society which is both free and unified. [1]

There are several reasons why Auden's speech and its sentiments are relevant to my consideration of Ward and the Adelphi Players. I must make clear, however, that there was no obviously shared ground between Auden and Ward. Indeed, Ward stated in 1942 that, 'the plays of Auden and Isherwood seem to have been abortive' and that 'the Unity Theatre had died of propaganda'. Nevertheless, there are some interesting if oblique connections between the two writers. Auden, seeking to widen opportunities for the publication of his poetry, had contacted Max Plowman, the editor of *The Adelphi* magazine, in 1930 with the result that some of Auden's verse was published in the magazine twelve months later. This was a significant stage in Auden's development in that it represented the first time that his poems had been published in a literary magazine with a national reputation.

---

1. W. H. Auden, "The Future of English Poetic Drama" in *Plays and other Dramatic Writings by W. H. Auden* edited by Edward Mendelson (Faber and Faber, 1989) p.521.

   As Cecil Davies makes clear in his opening chapter, Max Plowman and *The Adelphi* were central and crucial to Ward and the origins of the Adelphi Players. The Company's initial base was at The Adelphi Centre, a pacifist/socialist community run, at that time, by Max Plowman. The Centre had been established by John Middleton Murry as a non-sectarian experiment in community living which welcomed any socialists who were sympathetic to its basic ethos. He envisaged that the community living at the Centre would revolve around a relatively permanent nucleus of twelve persons, half of whom would be employed and have some form of economic security, and the other half working-class unemployed. It was at the invitation of Plowman that Ward and his Company were invited to use the Centre, also known as The Oaks, for their rehearsal and touring base.

   Ward and Plowman had met through their mutual involvement in the Peace Pledge Union in 1936. *The Adelphi* had begun publication in 1923 as a monthly literary journal under the editorship of Middleton Murry, specifically as a platform for D. H. Lawrence. The journal ran until 1955 and included contributions from Auden, Yeats, Eliot, Day-Lewis and Orwell.

   Ward also contributed to *The Adelphi,* and in January 1941 an article appeared by him entitled "The Theatre of Persons". Auden's concern for the nature of theatre and its relationship to 'man in relation to nature' is echoed in Ward's manifesto article:

> ... "theatre of persons" ... is a theatre which offers its audiences experience, the experience, first and foremost, of seeing themselves face to face. The real function of theatre is one of illumination, the casting of light upon the familiar, so that it is seen fully and for what it is ... in a word, the theatre must be seen in terms of persons; the transformed theatre must be a theatre of human beings, run by human beings for the sake of other human beings. [2]

It was the concept and ethos of the "Theatre of Persons" that was to inspire and inform the formation of the original Adelphi Players. Within his account of the three theatre Companies that toured – and finally settled – under the Adelphi name, Cecil Davies constantly refers back to his understanding of that ideal, and practice, of the Theatre of Persons. Later in this introduction, I shall discuss, in more detail, the implications of Ward's ideas.

   As I have already made clear, I do not wish to stretch tenuous comparisons between Ward and Auden. Nevertheless, in order to fully appreciate Ward's thinking and the context in which he formed the Adelphi Players, it is essential to broaden one's analysis of "The Pink Thirties", as Ronald Blythe refers to the period in his collection of essays about that pre-war decade, *The Age of Illusion*. Auden's passing engagement with Marxism and Ward's involvement

---

2.   R. H. Ward "The Theatre of Persons", *The Adelphi* (1941) pp.22–6 (p.122).

with both the Independent Labour Party and, more particularly, the Peace Pledge Union, offer helpful focal points to both their own creative output and the wider background context of the broad left Popular Front.

In both his manifesto article and the formation of the Adelphi Players, Ward's motivating concerns were always, I believe, a paradoxical mix of both the ethical and the pragmatic. As a playwright, most especially with his *Holy Family* (which he wrote for the Players), his work falls very interestingly into the genre of religious verse drama. In this important respect, another significant aspect of Auden's 1938 speech was its title: "The Future of English Poetic Drama". It is important to recall the significance and influence of that genre in British theatre of both the 1930s and the immediate, pre-1956, post-war period. In his account of The Group Theatre of London in the thirties, *Dances of Death*, Michael Sidnell observes that:

> Confusingly, political and religious drama often had much in common in motive and techniques. Hence Auden's equivocally Marxist *The Dance of Death* and Eliot's unequivocally Christian *The Rock* were bracketed together as products of a new school of playwrights. [3]

Sidnell's identification of both the diversity of ideological motivation and the commonality of form and style characterises much of the theatrical experimentation of the period. Throughout the 1930s, there remained a rich interplay of artistic experimentation across the arts.

As I have already acknowledged, Ward's most significant and, effectively, his most interesting, play was *Holy Family*, which Cecil Davies discusses in his account of the Adelphi Players. I offer some reflections on my evaluation of the play in my commentary notes to Chapter Two. Whilst I question whether Ward's play is as significant as Davies asserts in his own account of *Holy Family*, I certainly feel that it represents an interesting, if neglected, example of experimental verse drama, and one worthy of wider consideration.

In addition to the significance and interest of Ward as a verse dramatist, the Adelphi Players also merit interest and attention for their contribution to the clamour for artistic and structural reform within British theatre at that period. In their commitment to an ethical theatre of service and integrity, they contributed to, and were a part of, the broader movement within the non-commercial theatre towards a more progressive, artistically accountable and democratic theatre. This movement, discussed so cogently in Rowell and Jackson's *The Repertory Movement*, had its roots in the reforms sought by Shaw, Granville-Barker, Archer and others at the turn of the century.

---

3. Michael Sidnell, *Dances of Death: The Group Theatre of London in the Thirties* (London, Faber and Faber, 1984) p.35.

As Rowell and Jackson assert:

> Already at the turn of the century, the idea of repertory – as a form of theatre opposed in every way to the dominant commercial theatre of the time – had become an integral part of the developing concern with the future of theatre in Britain . . . At the same time, awareness was growing of the theatre's potency as an educative as well as artistic or entertainment medium, and therefore of its importance in the cultural life of the country as a whole. [4]

In an important sense, these central concerns identified by Rowell and Jackson were also primary motivations to the thinking and practice of practitioners such as Richard Ward. Ward spoke of the theatrical establishment as 'a garish and showy façade, reared upon the shifting sands of fashion'. Amongst others in the pre-war period who sought to challenge this complacent theatrical orthodoxy were Terence Gray at the Cambridge Festival Theatre, Peter Godfrey and later Norman Marshall at The Gate, Sir Barry Jackson's Birmingham Rep and, perhaps most memorably, Lilian Baylis at the Old Vic. There were also, of course, Rupert Doone and The Group Theatre, Ashley Dukes and his Mercury Theatre, and the politically-inspired Unity and Left theatre companies.

One important principle shared by these companies, including Ward's Adelphi Players, was a commitment – at least in their early phases – to perform plays in repertoire which were of artistic and ethical value but which would not find a platform within the commercial theatre of the West End. In a programme/prospectus circulated by the Adelphi in 1943 they expressed this sentiment in formal terms:

> It is becoming increasingly evident that the people of Britain feel the need and value of their cultural heritage in the darkness of the present. Where the theatre is concerned, there is clear and growing demand, not only for plays which will provide entertainment . . . but more especially for plays which are essentially re-creative in the sense of building up the human mind and spirit.

This climate of the need for progressive developments within cultural forms and audiences was an integral part of the broader ethos of oppositional thought and action in the period. Victor Gollancz, publisher of Ward's novels, was a significant influence through his formation of The Left Book Club and its accompanying magazine, *Left News*; other literary journals, along with this and *The Adelphi*, included *New Atlantis* and Claud Cockburn's *The Week*. In this same period, the Communist Party of Great Britain grew from just over a thousand members in 1930 to more than fifteen thousand by the close

---

4.   George Rowell and Anthony Jackson, *The Repertory Movement: A History of Regional Theatre in Britain* (Cambridge University Press, 1984) p.2.

of the decade. Meanwhile, at Oxford, the Reverend Dick Shepherd was establishing the Peace Pledge Union, an increasingly active and eloquent platform for the expression of broadly leftist, anti-militaristic and pacifist thinking. Shepherd's formation of the PPU in 1936 represented the significant embodiment of an ideological and ethical movement which had its origins in the interactive debate between oppositional Christian theology and socialism from the turn of the century. As I have previously noted, Ward met Max Plowman through the PPU, and Ward himself was a close friend and personal assistant to Shepherd and was very active in the early weeks and months of the movement. When Ward formed the Adelphi Players in May 1941, the male actors within the Company, including Ward himself, were all conscientious objectors.

In addition to his articles for *The Adelphi*, Ward was also a regular contributor to the PPU's weekly newspaper *Peace News*. In one such article, Ward asserted that 'War is not a disease which breaks out here and there in history, but the symptom of a disease which is the actual condition of the present social order, other symptoms of which, capitalism and imperialism, are inseparable from it and from one another. It is in effect against this unholy trinity – capitalism, imperialism and war – that the pacifist struggles.'

In the context of this radical analysis of the conditions which created the crisis leading up to the outbreak of war in 1939, it is perhaps surprising that Ward's own theatre activities were not more agitational in the manner of companies such as the Unity. Nevertheless, Ward's view of theatre was much more ethical and philosophical than ideologically agit-prop. When he argues for a 'transformed theatre . . . of human beings, run by human beings and for the sake of human beings', he is drawing upon his interest in Hegelian ethics and Jungian analytical psychology. The same ethical concern for 'persons', that characterises much of Ward's work with the Adelphi Players, features in another article for *Peace News* published just before the outbreak of the war: 'The world is what we make it, and when we refuse to be human beings, to be persons and treat others as persons, we make it hell.' These sentiments are especially interesting in the Adelphi's production of Marlowe's *Dr Faustus* to which Cecil Davies gives thoughtful attention in his text.

Whilst not all of the Company necessarily shared Ward's precise convictions, what does emerge in Davies' account of the Adelphi Companies is a theatre informed and characterised by a profound integrity and commitment. Fortunately the involvement of conscientious objectors with the Company was recognised by the Tribunals as "War Work", the equivalent for many other COs of land labour, ambulance work, etc. The combination of persons with diversely motivated anti-war convictions, along with the unique venture of taking theatre to new venues and audiences, undeniably helped to define the progressive outlook of the Adelphi. In their insistence upon equal salaries for all Company members, the shared distribution of tasks and responsibilities and the regular, open Company Meetings, the Adelphi prefigured some of the significant developments that were to emerge

through many of the theatre cooperatives and experimental companies of
the later post-war period.

In the Minutes of a Company Meeting dated 18 January 1942, Ward is
quoted as follows:

> The time is coming when our own age must evolve, out of its own soul, its own
> theatre – and by theatre, I mean its own plays, its own methods of acting and
> presentation. So far as I can see, our day has no theatrical heart . . .

Working on a very limited budget and performing almost exclusively in non-
theatre venues, including air raid shelters and open-air locations in the pre-
Adelphi Guild phase, it is remarkable that the Adelphi managed to achieve
the commendable standards of performance which, often, they undoubtedly
did. Ward and, eventually, Maurice Browne were working primarily with
inexperienced actors in conditions that did not easily allow for 'actor-training'
or growth. Cecil Davies offers the reader an invaluable, first-hand insight
into both those practical conditions and considerations which defined the
Adelphi years. In doing so he presents us with a perspective which, I believe,
in its immediate and personal response to that creative enterprise offers one
the necessary counterweight to the complementary discussion of the wider
context of social and cultural history. Therefore the incidental, day-to-day
details of lodging with an array of well-wishers (their audiences), and the
problems presented by constantly changing, non-specialist venues, possess
an importance for understanding the wider issues of touring theatre.

In my editorial approach, I have sought to respect and retain the integrity
of Cecil Davies' original manuscript, written over fifty years ago. In doing
so, I have tried to avoid the editor's unique access to the broader perspective
of hindsight. Consequently I have endeavoured to retain some examples of
the anecdotal and commonplace which must characterise the daily existence
of a Company such as the Adelphi Players. The tightrope-walk between
appropriate scholarly analysis and objectivity and the insights afforded by
the primary-source subjective requires delicate balance and negotiation.

It is my hope that this introduction and my notes within the chapters
succeed in maintaining that balance between the autonomy of Davies' view
and the contextualising of that perspective. In this way it is my belief that
the value of both the manuscript and the Companies themselves will be better
appreciated.

In the context of Richard Ward's understanding of theatre as something
of inherent value to persons and their communities, he and the Adelphi
embodied a faith in theatre, and its broader relationship towards progressive
social change, which may now seem remotely principled, if idealistic, from
our perspective of British society and culture at the beginning of a new
millennium.

In their breaking of new ground in terms of venues and audiences, I would
argue that the Adelphi played a small, but significant, part in helping to

create the social and cultural conditions which facilitated the growth of regional and community theatre after the war. As Cecil Davies himself says in his final chapter, only a relatively small number of people from the Adelphi moved into the wider world of professional theatre in the post-war period. Nevertheless some of those who did, such as Wilfred Harrison, went on to make significant contributions through companies such as the unique Century Theatre and the Octagon Theatre, Bolton, where Harrison was Artistic Director from 1971 to 1984.

In 1947, Richard Ward wrote that:

> I think we did begin to discover new ways of writing, producing and acting plays, rather as if we began to peel away the old theatre, much of it corrupt and deathly, and caught sight of a new one underneath.
>
> Whether we managed to put across that new theatre is another matter, and whether anyone, moved by our example, will follow us, is also another matter. But one or two things are certain; there is a vast audience for intelligent plays which have something to say to human persons, and there is a vast need for new ways of saying it. [5]

*

In terms of the structure and presentation of Cecil Davies' manuscript, I have retained his original chapter headings, although Chapter 5 represents the merging of two smaller chapters from the original version. I have also kept the terms "Producer" which has, of course now, metamorphosed into "Director".

With respect to the use of photographic evidence, I have sought, as editor, to offer a broad chronological overview of the various phases of Adelphi work. I hope that the photographs which I have selected indicate something of the development of the work whilst also conveying their own sense of theatre. Cecil Davies and I have endeavoured to identify and trace all photographers. However, owing to the time that has elapsed since the photographs were taken and the transient conditions of touring and 'life-on-the-road' in which they were kept, it has not proved possible to credit the photographer for all of those selected. Our apologies, therefore, to anyone whom we have inadvertently failed to acknowledge in this respect.

Peter Billingham

---

5.   R. H. Ward. "The Adelphi Players: A Tabloid History", *Peace News*, 29 August 1947, p.5.

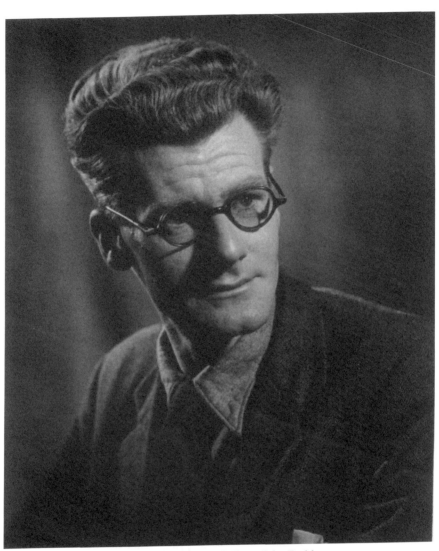

1. Richard Heron Ward. Photo: John Dodds

PROLOGUE

The Companies whose work forms the substance of this book were not famous, they contained no stars; they were not hailed as innovative and experimentalists; yet to thousands of people in scores of places all over the British Isles, they brought a new kind of theatre. This theatre may have been imperfect, even by their own particular standards, but still new, a theatre speaking to the condition of men and women in a way that the orthodox theatre was, and is still, failing to do.

It was no accident that it was in wartime that R. H. Ward formed the Adelphi Players through which to realise his vision of a Theatre of Persons. In modern war, that denial of the person which is latent in many aspects of society, emerges nakedly, and consequently the value of personality is felt more acutely. Most of the Company were inexperienced, many of their early performances must have been shocking. Yet from the beginning, the work, because of the values it expressed, however crudely, was precious to its audience who were often, indeed, embarrassing in their praise.

Gradually experience was gained and by orthodox standards the Company, and later still, Companies, became much 'better'. Whether they were in fact 'better', is another matter. When, years later, the last Company ceased working, it was not because it had become 'worse' by ordinary critical criteria, but because the initial impetus of the underlying vision had become weak.

Evolutionary patterns of thought are so firmly traced in the minds of most of us today that we forget that it is not for nothing that all myth looks back to the Age of Gold, or that Athene sprang fully-grown from the head of Zeus. We mistake elaboration for development, and sophistication for progress. The nature of things is otherwise, and the Theatre of Persons is, inevitably, rooted in the nature of things. The useful life of any particular phase of theatre history is limited. However, the soul of the enterprise, the vision itself, awaits incarnation.

Thus, though the Companies no longer exist, the book about them is worth writing. We shall see what kind of Companies these were, what sort of plays they chose, how they acted them, what sort of people formed the Companies, what sort of audiences saw them, and through these details attempt to form a picture of a theatre based on human personality.

1

A DEMOCRATIC ORGANISM

Planned for some time before, the original company calling itself 'The Adelphi Players' was founded early in 1941 by R. H. Ward, and began its first period of rehearsal at The Oaks, Langham, near Colchester on 12 May 1941.

The choice of name and headquarters are important. Not only the general appropriateness of the name in its original meaning of 'Brothers' caused it to be used, but also the inspiration of one of the great men of the first half of the twentieth century, Max Plowman.

R. H. Ward had known Max Plowman since 1936, and shared with him a vision of life which drew the two men close together, though Max Plowman was about twice Ward's age. At the time of the Company's foundation Max Plowman was editing *The Adelphi* magazine from The Adelphi Centre, at The Oaks. This centre, originally founded as The Adelphi School Company by John Middleton Murry and others for the study and practice of Socialism in association with *The Adelphi* magazine, had later been used to house fifty Basque children, refugees from the Spanish Civil War. After their departure and the outbreak of war, Max Plowman took a band of like-minded people to The Oaks to put the place in order, do market-gardening and look after aged evacuees. In spite of the closeness of the tie between them, Ward felt unable to join Plowman in this venture. He had already had a bad taste of community living in his own experimental Abbey Gardens Community and feared the same faults might develop at The Oaks.

When Ward began to see clearly that his next task was to form a special kind of theatrical company, however, it was in harmony with what had gone before, that Plowman should offer him The Adelphi Centre as a rehearsal base. Indeed, the formation of the Company and its association with his own work at the Centre, was an indirect fulfilment of Max Plowman's life-long passion for the theatre and the longing he had often felt to start some sort of 'Barn Theatre' of his own.

In the January 1941 issue of *The Adelphi* magazine appeared an essay by R. H. Ward entitled 'The Theatre of Persons'. This essay was the first public event in our story and, as it was in effect a manifesto of the kind of theatre Ward hoped to develop, we shall often have to refer to it. Thus, through the personal relationship between Max Plowman and Richard Ward, the new company became the Adelphi Players.

During the first weeks of rehearsal, Max died. As Warden of the Centre came Joe Watson from the blast furnaces of Consett. Middleton Murry once more became editor of the magazine.

Ward and Phoebe Waterfield had had experience of playing in London in 1940 with the Pilgrim Players (Oxford Company) [1] and for London, with its strange new life in shelters and with its unexpected air raids, the new Company was designed. It inherited some costumes and properties, and initially some personnel from an amateur company: the Adelphi Group with which Ward had been earlier associated.

To London, then, using a little van loaned by a well-wisher, the Company moved when its first two productions were rehearsed, and for about eight months operated primarily there. As the situation in London became easier, short tours revealed demands elsewhere, and in March 1942 a provincial tour of six weeks initiated a period in which London 'seasons' of lessening scope alternated with tours.

The very first long tour included a visit to Ilkley Playhouse which, later, with the cooperation of its owners – the Ilkley Players – was to be for some time the headquarters of the Company.

Another tour involved the experiment of working in conjunction with Local Authorities in their plans of entertainment for 'Holidays at Home'. Meanwhile, the centre of gravity was moving north. In September 1942 the Company rehearsed, for the last time, at The Oaks, and in November for the first time at Ilkley.

On 1 June 1943, during rehearsals at Ilkley of Ward's play *Robin Hood*, growing internal frictions exploded, as a result of which Ward and three others tendered their resignations, to take effect at the end of the season: 7 September 1943. Through the intervention of Maurice Browne, however, who arrived in the midst of all of this to produce *The Duchess of Malfi* by John Webster, these resignations were withdrawn. By the end of July it was decided that Ward should form a small Company with complete freedom of action within the Adelphi framework, primarily to do 'rural' tours. At the end of this season, this decision was implemented and the 'Second' Company came into being, whose history, being shorter than that of the 'First' Company, we shall follow first.

The Second Company

With four members only, and a production so simple that its material properties could, metaphorically, be carried in a suitcase, this Company, using a car and two-wheeled trailer, toured until early 1945. At this stage, the policy

---

1.   There were two Pilgrim Players companies, formed almost simultaneously at the outbreak of war. The Oxford Pilgrim Players were founded by Ruth Spalding, active in the Religious Drama Society (better known as RADIUS), which Bishop George Bell had founded in the nineteen twenties. The aim of this society was to promote religious drama of the highest quality artistically, whilst promoting a more diverse and liberal interpretation of the nature of 'Religious Drama'. Elliot Martin Browne (1900–80) was appointed as the first Drama Advisor for RADIUS and it was he, who, along with his wife – the actress Henzie Raeburn – founded the better-known Canterbury Pilgrim Players who toured throughout the war years.

[of the Second Company] was considerably altered. The Company was enlarged. The car and trailer sold, a thirty-two-seater bus was bought which could carry the Company and rather more elaborate (though still very simple) productions, and the plan was to carry four plays (to be produced by Maurice Browne) on a tour of one-week stands. This was to be called the Second Company's International Season. Eventually a nine-week rehearsal period (without Maurice Browne) was followed by a tour with three plays. The final production by the Second Company was to put on its production of Raynal's *The Unknown Warrior* at the Lindsey Theatre, Notting Hill Gate.

The season following this was planned as a special Schools' Season. What would have been a very interesting scheme had been worked out by which the Company 'invaded' a school for the day with a series of lectures and demonstrations, culminating in a short performance. Unfortunately for the Company, schools did not appreciate such interference with routine, nor do Local Education Authorities, or Private or Independent schools lightly pay out the twenty guineas which the Company calculated was the minimum fee possible for the scheme. As a consequence, when only a few days were left before the next season was due to begin, there were only two engagements and little likelihood of more. Funds being low, the Company tired, the future uncertain, the Company wound up.

The First Company

Meanwhile, the original, First Company, directed by J. Boyd Brent had established a pattern of work: rehearsal period, tour, holiday, which was steadily maintained throughout 1944 and 1945. The number of plays in stock was kept at about three.

Individual members of the Company, however, hoped for a more stable life than that of continuous touring, and on artistic grounds it was felt that a regional system would be more satisfactory, and would be in harmony with what was then the Arts Council's policy of regionalisation. [2] For some time,

---

2. The Arts Council of Great Britain was formally constituted in August 1946, building upon its predecessor CEMA: the Council for the Encouragement of Music and the Arts. CEMA had been founded at the beginning of 1940 with the aid of grants from the Pilgrim Trust and from the Treasury, to bring concerts and plays to the crowded evacuation centres. It represented the first State involvement in, and financial support for, the Arts. In its Royal Charter, the ACGB had the object of 'developing a greater knowledge, understanding and practice of the fine arts exclusively, and in particular, to increase the accessibility of the fine arts to the public.' The Adelphi Players had received some financial help from CEMA. In 1945, the Government had produced a White Paper on 'Community Centres', recognising the achievements of the non-commercial, independent theatre activities during wartime. One of the first initiatives of the newly formed ACGB after the war was to encourage and press for the development of regionally-based theatres. With the cessation of war and the attempt by the authorities to resume more stable economic and cultural conditions, this decision reflected a move away from the support of touring companies, towards a structure that would facilitate the rebuilding of communities in the immediate post-war period.

the Company had been planning to centre themselves in a region, and everything pointed to the Potteries as the place for the experiment. The Autumn of 1946 was fixed for the start of this scheme, and meanwhile, partly as a step towards it, and partly because it seemed a good idea intrinsically, the Company played its 'Special Cornish Season'. For four months from 17 May to 13 September 1946, using Camborne as a base, the Company played in nine Cornish towns. In each of these, in cooperation with the local Arts and Music Societies, it presented in approximately four, monthly visits, the whole repertory of the season. This consisted initially of two plays. Four others were rehearsed during the season. It was a successful, though tiring, scheme.

The Cornish Season over, the Company moved to the city of Stoke-on-Trent, where it hoped to establish a permanent regional theatre. It failed to do so for one reason only: namely that a satisfactory Headquarters could not be found.

A Miners' Hostel originally thought of was found to be badly situated and inconvenient. The only rehearsal rooms that could eventually be found had no provision for sewing or stage work. There was no regular place in which productions could be opened. Regretfully the Company looked elsewhere, still seeking, however, to serve this area in some way.

Adelphi Guild Theatre

One of the most successful strands in this [touring] Circuit was Macclesfield where a lively Playgoers Society always packed the hall for every performance. There were, too, a number of individuals who were well-disposed to the Company and were prepared to go to a good deal of trouble to help them. As a result, arrangements were made by which the Brocklehurst Hall, used for performances, could be rented as a place of rehearsal. A workshop, not ideal, but usable, was found and rented not too far away. So on 12 February 1947, In the midst of the worst weather since 1940, the Company moved its headquarters to Macclesfield where it began yet another system of working: performing only one play at a time in Macclesfield and within the surrounding region (to Staffordshire in the South and up into Lancashire in the North) while another was, in the mornings, rehearsed and constructed.

This system, with occasional variations such as visits to Northern Ireland and to Cornwall, continued with Macclesfield as base, until the very end of the Company's existence.

The Company took this occasion to begin work under a new name: The Adelphi Guild Theatre. The old name was felt to imply a company of Strolling Players and it was a form of name so frequently used in the amateur theatre that it was felt advisable to change it. It was thought that the North Midlands Theatre Scheme [the Macclesfield-based scheme] would be better-served by a body calling itself a 'Theatre' than 'Players'. The word 'Guild', though not particularly original, kept clear and public the cooperative and democratic character of the Company. About this time the Company had to be formally constituted as a non-profit distributing company limited by guarantee, and into the wording of this constitution were incorporated, as far as possible, the working elements of the Company as it had existed. In fact it is impossible to express in legal phrases the spirit of such a company and when, later, friction called attention to the 'letter' [of the constitution], it was found to be capable of interpretation in ways far from the 'spirit'.

Indeed, by 1948, It was clear that a gulf was growing between the Director [J. Boyd Brent] and the majority of the Company, and as his formal re-election approached, it seemed likely that he would be voted out. However, by placing before the Company his long-term ideals and something of his short-term plans, he succeeded in convincing the members that he was still the right leader.

Before long, when concrete details of immediate policy began to emerge, many regretted that they had been so persuaded. Soon indeed, a crazy situation developed: the Director had power under the Constitution, to dismiss anyone from employment in the Company.

This did not, of course, affect their legal membership of the Limited Company. It had always been assumed that the 'legal' membership and the 'working' membership would roughly coincide. However, soon a situation arose in which a majority of the members of the Limited Company were no longer working with the Company, yet could do nothing to alter this situation until the next Annual General Meeting: nearly a year away. At the 1949 A.G.M. a fierce fight was expected, but quite quietly, the Director was outvoted and a new director, Seamus Stewart, elected. The previous Director and his Business Manager were deprived of Company membership altogether.

For about a year it appeared that the storm had been weathered but though the 1950–1 season began adventurously, the Company was unable to fight the financial difficulties it encountered and went into Voluntary Liquidation while there was still something for the creditors to have. There was rather a bitter irony, perhaps, in that the largest of these creditors was Piers Plowman, son of Max, whose inspiration had given so much to the Company's beginnings just ten years earlier.

For a year after this the Adelphi Guild Theatre remained in existence on paper, and was then finally dissolved.

In a sense [Richard Ward's concept of] 'Theatre of Persons' is tautological, for all theatre is, fundamentally, 'of Persons'. To concentrate on other aspects of it – spectacle, music, rhetoric – is to attend to the condiments, cookery and garnishings rather than to the vital food. But this is precisely what most modern theatre does do. Much effort in the theatre is directed towards perfecting non-essentials. Most critiques of theatrical productions deal with everything except the one that really matters.

The aim of the Adelphis was to create a theatre rightly proportioned, in which first things came first, even at the cost of their becoming Puritans of the theatre: avoiding many things not evil in themselves, which were obscuring the best.

I have often thought that R. H. Ward at this time was something of a George Fox of the theatre, though I doubt whether either would greatly like the comparison.[3] Fox in religion and Ward in the theatre emphasised the centrality of the individual human person, and the immediate relationship between that person and the eternal verities. Both found themselves dissatisfied with the established forms. Both opposed the formalists of their days and both abandoned outward elaborations in order to concentrate on inner realities. They also both created 'societies' which were experiments in organic democracy far superior to the political forms which existed in their own times. Finally, they both held firmly to ideals of simplicity: in both, a spiritual vision bore ethical fruit, and both – to the unsympathetic outsider – seemed to be damned awkward cusses: angular, arrogant and obtuse.

In an early Company Meeting, Ward said that the Theatre should be a fusion of Arts and Ethics. The statement is forbidding and suggests a pulpit-theatre of ideas, rather than of persons, didactic rather than entertaining. This impression is false but the statement demands amplification. Just as man cannot avoid theatre, so theatre cannot avoid ethics, for situations between persons – the stuff of theatre – involves conflicts of persons and conflicts within persons. Furthermore, the conflicts that matter to us most are the conflicts of right with wrong, of reason with passion. Such conflicts are seen in *Hamlet*, *Macbeth* or *Faust*.

Nor can the theatre be morally neutral. Theatre practitioners are playing upon an instrument whose notes are ethical, they may play in tune or out of tune, but play they must or shut up shop. The Theatre of Persons is *ipso facto* a theatre of values. The dramatist is, one way or another, a propagandist of his own sense of values. If this is false then his whole work will lack truth, his persons will be sham persons, his theatre bad theatre.

Ward, admitting he was restating Aristotle, wrote: "The theatre may, in fact, be an instrument for widening and deepening the consciousness of the individual; taken in conjunction with his own subjective experience, it may lead him to an imaginative condition in which his own life, and through it the lives of others, and nature generally, may be seen, understood and used".

---

3.   George Fox was the founder of the Religious Society of Friends, better-known as the Quakers. Founded in 1648–50, the Society of Friends originated and evolved in reaction to the perceived hypocrisy of much religious orthodoxy at that time. Unwilling to recognise the status or necessity of the function of the priest as an intermediary, Quakers have, instead, focused upon the autonomy and integrity of the individual's personal encounter and experience in spiritual matters. They meet in silent, shared, contemplative worship, where any person present may share their reflective thoughts and observations.

It would be absurd to suggest that the people Ward first gathered together were consciously filled with these ideas. They were very ordinary people, not all of whom had any real experience of theatre at all. Of those who had, only one, Phoebe Waterfield, could be called experienced.

A clergyman in Birmingham, during one of the early tours, said: "You people are performing religious plays. May I ask whether you are religious people?" to which Ward relied "If we were not we should not be doing this". The answer was just. Religiously, the Company was a mixed bag. There were Anglicans, there was one 'birth-right' Quaker, and varying degrees of non-conformity and agnosticism were represented. That was irrelevant. The motive-power of the Company was religious. The sense of dedication among the members was religious. Ward said at one Meeting that the Company should identify itself with the re-marriage of Art and Religion, divorced since the time of the Reformation. This identification, clearly apparent in the earlier years of the work, was perhaps the Company's greatest strength. Divorced from religion, the attempt to "Be a person and treat others like persons" (a quotation from Hegel to which Ward more than once drew attention) could have degenerated into a spineless humanism, but this did not happen.

It would be easy to idealise the first phase of Adelphi work if one had not been closely involved in it, and if its Director had not placed on record his sense of the Company's inadequacy. After the first performance in Church, he wrote:

> Last night the vicar, introducing us before the performance, shamed us considerably by saying that we in fact were what we know we ought to be and are not: a body of people banded together in self-dedication to the task of bringing the word of God to their fellow-men . . . We were told, too, that we had brought the spirit of St Francis of Assisi into that Church. It was not true. But perhaps it gives us a purpose. For there is a sense in which, whatever plays we perform and wherever we perform them, we may become Franciscans of a kind: poor men and women who, loving God in their fellows and their fellows in God, go from place to place, asking their livelihood and giving their lives . . . I say that this is a purpose . . . At present, we are failures if these are aspirations. But I say too that, unless some such aspiration at least is real to us, in these days and circumstances, we are no more than a burden upon our fellows' generosity.

In fact the value of the Company lay in what it actually was, and not in what it might become, for those aspirations, which Director said could justify its existence, became a part of its nature and gave meaning and value to work often pitifully inadequate and imperfect.

In July 1942, Richard Ward said that he thought that fairly soon, perhaps about the [First] Company's second birthday, the organisation should be wound up. He proposed this only in order to found another "of the same and yet of a different nature". [This separation was, in fact, the split and division that the author has previously referred to i.e. the formation of the short-lived Second Company and the involvement of Maurice Browne.] As time went on, the Adelphis tended more and more to live on the spiritual resources of their beginnings, and when these were largely exhausted, a moral vacuum was created into which new ideas and ideals flowed, often of a very different character.

This 'spiritual biography', understanding of which must precede real understanding of the outward story of plays and players, manifested itself most clearly in the story of internal organisation. To a large extent the internal shape of the Companies determined and made possible their particular kind and quality of performance. Few of the players having an orthodox theatrical background, they found everything novel, the life no less than the work. They were closely connected with people interested in communal living as such. The very word 'Community' was then something of a shibboleth in certain circles.[4] It was natural that they should at times see their work as an experiment in 'Community'. The Adelphi experiment was successful primarily because the life was designed to serve a common purpose which united the individuals and they deliberately avoided applying the 'Community' shibboleth to it.

The theatre is in some senses a microcosm of the world and those who seek to create a new theatre do so either because the world outside has changed, and is not properly expressed in the old theatre, or because they see the new theatre as part of a new world. The Adelphi Players were of the latter. The Theatre of Persons was to them only a part of an increasingly impersonal world, in which they had to seek out and respond to personal elements and endeavour to make their Company the model of a personal world. Thus the danger of losing sight of the professional aims of the Company is inherent in its nature, a weakness arising from its greatest strength, its refusal to treat the theatre in purely theatrical terms. The original Company was at first independent of outside bodies. From the start, the chief instrument of organisation was the Company Meeting.

This was attended by all Members and in it anything connected with the work and life of the Company could be discussed. At that first Meeting, held at the Barn rehearsal room, Langham, on Thursday 1 May 1941 at 10.30 am, Ward described the proposed nature of the Company. It was to have a cooperative basis, the privileges and responsibilities of members were to be equal, he himself was in a special position for the time as preliminary organiser and Director. The fundamental concepts expressed by the Director in that meeting gave the twig the bent which was found in the tree. They were never wholly lost sight of, and proved themselves to be in harmony

---

4.   Community was indeed a shibboleth of the period, although with considerably more progressive and radical connotations than its reactionary political usage in the Thatcherite nineteen-eighties. Middleton Murry's Adelphi Community was, therefore, an expression of wider radical initiatives of that time. I recommend George Ineson's *Community Journey* (London, Sheed and Ward, 1956) for those who would like to pursue this area in more detail.

with the artistic and social aims and usages of the personal theatre. The economic equality was never a flat egalitarianism. Salaries were equal, but economic equality did not extend beyond salaries. Thus as individuals in society the members enjoyed or suffered its natural inequalities, but within the Company all were paid the same. The small-part actor, stage manager, Director: all accepted the same financial return for their work. In this way the concept of the equal responsibility of members was translated into hard reality. Each member was in fact equally important to the work of the Company. No task was regarded as in any way inferior to another. It is impossible to lay too much stress on the importance of the equal salary principle. It was both a key-stone and a touchstone. An extraordinary sense of mutual confidence and helpfulness was engendered by the economic arrangements: that jealousy which is usually so marked a feature of backstage life alike in the professional and amateur theatre was absent. A further effect of the equal salaries was that they determined the kind of people who wished to join the Company.[5]

No one would join merely for money, for the equal salary was of necessity also extremely low. The ambitious could see that its framework offered no scope for mere self-advancement. All who joined had to possess some measure of humility and a readiness to accept something very near to poverty.

At the very beginning the equality was absolute: each person received £2 a week when the Company was playing, equal billeting privileges at The Oaks for rehearsal periods and equal holiday pay when any holiday could be found. The situation naturally grew more complex as time passed, though few of the complexities arose during the first two years. Two which did were that of part-time members, of whom the most important was Molly Sole, who laid the foundations of the business side of the Company, but did not become a full-time worker for three years. The other role was that of peripatetic tours managers. When Richard Bishop was engaged as tours manager in April 1942, we find in the minutes of the twenty eighth Company Meeting that this engagement raised the whole question of equal pay for all full-time members. At this same meeting it was agreed that all full-time members should receive £2 per week with equal bonuses or increments.

Many interesting sidelights are cast on the attitude to money matters that prevailed in the Company, and a few examples of how things worked in practice will be very illustrative of this. The weighing together of communal and private needs sometimes led to situations not without humour. In 1942, Jane Fitz-Gerald had been taken ill. Her place in Strindberg's *Easter* had been temporarily taken by Mrs Plowman, Max's widow. Her son, Piers, was a member of the Company by this time.

---

5. Equal Salaries: The Adelphi Players were not quite unique in this respect. For example, Martin Browne's Pilgrim Players had also instituted what they called the "Tommy Rate" of £2 per week, so-called because this was the infantryman's weekly wage during wartime.

Mrs Plowman, while accepting the salary, had refused to allow the Company to pay her rail fares. The treasurer had therefore seen fit to pay her lodgings bill without her knowledge. Piers Plowman was requested not to mention this in the quarters most concerned. The well-intentioned subterfuge was not wholly successful, and in minutes of the next meeting it was reported that Mrs Plowman sent the Company fourteen shillings "for a celebration".

In the same minutes we read that it was to be left to individual members to claim from Petty Cash what they felt they needed as a result of certain heavy lodgings bills. This adjustment of lodgings expenses was only one of many. When the original eight first went to London some had lodgings and some hospitality at home or with relatives. It was therefore agreed that members not paying for lodgings should pay one eighth each of the lodgings expenses of the others. Hospitality was frequently provided through the generosity of the local organisers of performances, and particular hardships were given special attention. Much was left to the individual conscience and so closely were the members united that consciences were exceptionally sensitive. The sums so seriously discussed and weighed in these transactions must seem absurdly small. The whole enterprise was 'capitalised', by two generous friends one of whom lent a small van, the other £50 interest-free. In February 1942, the situation arose that the assets of the Company, including money owed to it, amounted to £64 whilst its debts were approximately £89. It emerged that the accounts were carried in the Director's name. There was no limited liability or other protection for him, and he foresaw the possibility of having his furniture sold to pay the debts. Then one of those things happened which those of us who were long with the Company came to call 'Adelphi'.

Jack Boyd Brent said that he had capital amounting to about £150 (most of us were penniless) which he was prepared, in the event of a real emergency, to put at the Company's disposal. Ward declared that as long as that spirit existed he had no fears as to their future. I believe that was the only time that Ward referred to the great additional responsibility he bore in the Company.

In the meetings of the Adelphi Players, voting was rare and resorted to only when some clear-cut and inescapable issue had failed to be decided by the 'sense of the meeting': normally it was that 'sense' of the meeting' that determined what ought to be done.[6] When the method is practised completely as it is among the Quakers, there is not a fixed motion, formulated beforehand, which imprisons discussion in a form of words. Instead, the

---

6.   Sense of the Meeting: In accordance with the open and democratic form of Meeting employed by the Religious Society of Friends, agreement on issues relating to individual judgement and shared belief is sought mutually by those present at any given meeting. This discerned, 'sense' of a Meeting, is undertaken through quiet and patient contemplation within the framework and guidance of the publication *Quaker Faith and Practice*. The 'sense' of a Meeting is difficult to quantify but, in principle, allows for the collective and democratic involvement of all present.

'motion' emerges from the discussion. It is true that after the first phase, Adelphis tended more to 'propose motions' in meetings, but when this became normal it indicated how far from their origins they had moved.

Company meetings could go on for ever and business was urgent, so that where the Quakers could carry a minute forward a month, a quarter or a year, the Adelphis had to decide immediately on actions involving all. So the 'sense of the meeting' was found to be not what the majority would have decided but what the majority were prepared to try because it was the opinion of a minority of recognised wisdom. Such a democracy, however, depended for its development on the prior growth of mutual understanding and trust. This was clear to Ward. On the first occasion when he had to dismiss a member, he simply took the appropriate action and then announced to the Company what he had done.

Someone then raised the question of whether the dismissal of a member for any reason should be effected without previous discussion. This was at a very early date, only twenty five days, in fact, after the first Meeting.

To the divided Company came Maurice Browne who quickly assumed effective leadership of the divided Adelphi Players and in the 'second phase' (1 June – 7 September 1943) he is the dominant figure.[7] Ward was too weary and Brent too inexperienced in Direction to do other than accept his predominance. The former, persuaded to withdraw his resignation, became one of a strange triumvirate as Director in perpetuity with Browne and Brent as elected directors. Only one Meeting of this triumvirate is recorded, and within a fortnight the minutes record that "the three directors stated that they believed the best way of conducting company business was not to have separate director's meetings and member's meetings but to one meeting of all members".

At the meeting which elected the uneasy triumvirate, Browne advanced a statement, accepted by the Company, in which three 'principles' were established. This same meeting of 19 June is remarkable also for the fact that, with the Chair taken by Browne, the business was conducted as a series of formal motions, proposed, seconded, and voted upon. The Minutes are utterly unlike any other Adelphi Minutes before or after, for the very next day, 20 June, at the only recorded meeting of the three directors it was – rather ironically "Agreed that voting procedure be abandoned in either Company meetings or Director's meetings whenever humanly possible, and that decisions in both cases be reached by a general sense of the Company or the directors."

---

7.   Maurice Browne (1881–1955) was an experienced English actor, director and theatre manager. Credited with the founding of the Little Theatre movement, he is also remembered for producing R.C. Sherriff's ground-breaking *Journey's End* in 1929. He is also remembered for his production of *Othello* at the Savoy Theatre in 1930, with Paul Robeson in the title role, Peggy Ashcroft as Desdemona and Browne himself playing Iago. He had 'retired' from the theatre in 1939.

A gradual concentration of power in the Director's hands began in 1943 and ended in the constitution of the Adelphi Guild Theatre in 1947, by which, as is discussed earlier in this chapter, the Director was given enormous powers during his year of office. During the 'Interim Season' that followed Maurice Browne's coming, the difference between the minority and majority groups crystallised in terms of policy. From the very beginning the Company had known that its work and aims could be viewed from two perspectives: artistic and social. To present 'persons to persons' was an aim at once artistic and ethical involving certain artistic methods and a certain attitude to the audience, including the ways in which, and the places where, the audience was sought. The synthesis of these two aspects had never been easy to maintain. Under the strain of dissension and perhaps also because of, rather than in spite of Browne's guidance, the synthesis largely broke down. A long complex company meeting was held on 30 and 1 July 1943 on the first day of which Ward reaffirmed his earlier desire to leave at the end of the season. "Considerable discussion was held on the possibilities of the company dividing so as to do both more rural work and work of its present kind." In fact, the three foundation members of the Second Company constituted themselves as at first as co-equal Directors and employed one other person, though later Ward became sole director. Throughout its history this Company, as revealed in its Minutes, carried on the traditions of the original Company. Latterly the equal salaries were supplemented by Family Allowances which made it possible for men with wives and families to be employed.

2
THE PLAYS

In a review of the aims of the original company at an Extraordinary Meeting held in January 1942, Ward classified under three very broad headings the kinds of plays which should form the repertory of the Theatre of Persons:

1) *Neo-Elizabethan*, which he explained as the revival of Elizabethan drama played under conditions and in a manner approximating to those which existed in Shakespeare's day, and also contemporary drama written in a similar form.

2) *Odd Plays*, by which he meant productions such as *Holy Family*, a play of his own which was at that time in the repertory and which was a new departure in dramatic conception.

3) *Intimate Plays* such as had been written by Strindberg and certain other playwrights for performance to small audiences under conditions that brought them into closer and more intimate touch with the actors than the usual large West End theatres afforded.

The validity of this rough classification was largely borne out in Adelphi practice. Although in the Adelphi Guild Theatre phase, the original concept was somewhat overlaid and a number of plays produced which would have found no place earlier, we may say that the ideal never ceased, largely, to influence the choice of plays.

At the time of the statement [of criteria for Repertoire] the Company had five productions to its credit and one projected. These first six productions were:

- Five of Laurence Housman's *Little Plays of St Francis* (Brother Elias, Brother Ass, Brother Sin, Holy Disobedience and The Fool's Errand.)
- A shortened version of Marlowe's *Tragical History of Dr Faustus*
- Laurence Housman's *Abraham and Isaac*
- Richard Ward's *Holy Family*
- A short medley entitled *The Actors are at Hand*
- Strindberg's *Easter*.

Housman's *Little Plays* would not, I think, be claimed by anyone as 'great' drama. They are true to their title. Not only are they brief, but many have small casts, always a determining factor in Adelphi work. They make small demands in the way of staging and properties. The first publicity leaflet of the Company said:

The Players are willing to give performances at any time of day and in any place, indoors or outdoors, where there is room for their audience and themselves. They carry their own equipment and provide their own publicity material.

The extreme simplicity of Housman's plays was therefore a great recommendation. They proved also suitable material for 'apprentices', negatively in their slight technical demands, positively in the genuine humanity of their characters and situations. They were in harmony, also, with Ward's desire to re-marry Art and Religion: in themselves unassuming, their central theme religious, the persons in them portrayed with that spiritual dimension without which humanity is incomplete.

The Little Plays were kept in the repertory for five months, during which they were performed sixty five times. Then they were dropped, the demand for them was not exhausted, but dropped they were. The players' jocular name for them – 'The Little Plagues' – reflected a growing staleness.

Dr Faustus, the second production, was in the repertory for other reasons and presented problems and opportunities of a different kind. In Ward's article on the 'Theatre of Persons' in *The Adelphi* (January 1941) we read:

> The theatre is finally an allegory, and must be so treated by those who work in it; it puts new words and new dresses things that we all know, and by its vividness, and even its sensationalism, brings to the human mind, often by shock methods, comprehension of things so ordinary, so deeply rooted in nature and history, that we pass them by as too familiar to notice. As the life of Christ is an allegory of what all human life may be and much human life unconsciously is, and for that reason holds us even in spite of ourselves, so the stories of the great plays – *Faust, Hamlet, Macbeth, Oedipus* – are stories of ourselves, revealing us for our own understanding.

It is in terms of allegory that the theatre must be seen; it must concern itself with plays about essentials and the persons in whom they are vested.

The *Faust* story, then, was one of the great stories of the theatre which it was Ward's deepest and most urgent desire to set upon the stage. As it stands in the early editions (the Quarto of 1604 was actually the basis of the version used) this drama does not seem to promise well for the small Company anxious to play only the best. Richard Ward's shortened version was a clean and clear-cut play, impressive in the simplicity of its pattern, and probably far nearer to Marlowe's original conception than the corrupt versions that have come down to us.

In this version too, the cast was brought within the Company's limits and the greater part of it consisted of those magnificent dialogues between Faustus and Mephistopheles which form the core of the play. The 'Neo-Elizabethan' production demanded for furniture only a suitable table and chair, and very few properties, of which the bulkiest and heaviest were the Doctor's books. Thus, apart from the two items of furniture, which the organisers of performances were asked to provide, this production could be carried by the actors to the place of performance. *Dr Faustus* entered very deeply into the Adelphi consciousness and remains even now as one of those half-dozen or so of plays that seem to symbolize the primary values of the Companies. *Faustus* is a 'symbol' of Modern Man: Renaissance Man. The primary characteristic of the modern world is pursuit of power through knowledge, an unholy alliance leading to the Hydrogen Bomb, Nagasaki, Hiroshima and Napalm.

There are some greater plays but none which could, In 1941, speak more clearly, more vividly, or more truly, to the condition of men and women suffering the very fruits of that application of the pursuit of knowledge to the achievement of power that the play portrayed.

The third production (August 1941) was Housman's *Abraham and Isaac*. Although introduced into the repertoire nearly three months before *Little Plays* were dropped, this was, in effect their successor. It remained in stock until November 1942, and was twice revived for brief periods, once in 1943, and once in 1944. The Players were privileged to be given the first production rights of this play, so that from a very early date they were putting into practice a principle which, although never stated explicitly, was tacitly recognised by them as of importance – that of bringing new plays into the theatre. The Adelphi Players knew that it is the dramatists who provide the life-blood of the theatre, and that dramatists cannot write unless their plays are sometimes performed.

The most notable of these early productions was the first production of Ward's *Holy Family*.[1] Undoubtedly, this play was the most important 'event'

---

1.   *Holy Family* opened, for its second, revised production, at the Ilkley Playhouse on 23 November 1942 and was withdrawn on 24 April 1943, at the Civic Playhouse, Bradford, after a total of 79 performances. It was with this play that Ward sought to try and define the kind of play that might point toward the transformed theatre of the age: one which he anticipated emerging after the defeat of Fascism and the ending of the war. In style, it is in the genre of religious verse drama and incorporates an interesting stylistic device in having a Chorus who appear in multiple roles within the narrative of the play. The Nativity Story is transposed into a contemporary setting with the characters representing ordinary people of contemporary, wartime Britain. The play attracted controversy in some religious quarters, owing to Ward's emphasis upon the humanity, rather than the divinity, of Christ. Ward was eventually obliged to make amendments to the original script in order to try and limit criticism of the play and to ensure that it would continue to receive production. It was, therefore, this revised version which opened at Ilkley. There is a photograph of the Ilkley production on page 42. I believe that the play is of significant interest as an example of a dramatic genre which, up until the *annus mirabilis* of 1956, seemed likely to define the development of a New Writing in post-war British theatre. However, following on Osborne's success with *Look Back in Anger*, it was to be social realism as a genre and a left-tempered humanism that characterised the initial achievements of that theatre, rather than the Anglo-Catholic conservatism of Eliot, Duncan and Fry.

in the whole Adelphi history, and although the second production the following year was felt to be a far better one than the first, that first production simply by virtue of priority was in many ways the most fruitful thing that the company ever did.

In a Preface to the First Edition, Ward says:

> Just as the architect's plan seems to the inexpert to bear little relation to a finished building, so the script which follows may seem to bear little relation to a play seen upon the stage . . . Here nothing is offered but the words to be spoken.

In 1951, more than a hundred performances of this play were given by various people in various places in England, America and Australia. The play was, in the author's own words, "an experiment, written for a particular company and particular circumstances, and intended to do no more than supply a 'parochial' need". It was regarded at the time by many people as 'experimental' or 'queer' or 'high-brow' yet only ten years later, it was accepted as the sort of religious play that people do if they do religious plays at all.

Holy Family was, among other things, the author's response to the Company. The existence of the Company, its aims, the personalities in it, and the qualities it had begun to reveal, all contributed to the genesis, form and qualities of the play. Here was the fruitful union of author and theatre, the genuine creative intercourse of craftsmen that the Art of the Theatre always demands but rarely is given.

For all its hundred performances in 1951, it is too little known – yet it was written in 1941, long before *The Shadow Factory*, *The Old Man of the Mountains*, *This Way to the Tomb*: usually cited as the pioneer plays of a new poetic and religious drama. It was more revolutionary than these. *Murder in the Cathedral* stands there years before it, it is true, and here and there in Ward's verses are echoes of some of its rhythms. They are echoes only, and the pervading rhythms are as unlike Eliot as are the approaches to the central Christian mysteries in the play. In *Holy Family* we see a new form though its roots are in the pre-Aeschylean drama when the protagonists had not yet emerged from the Chorus.

For the cast of this play is a Chorus which may be regarded as an amorphous collection of men and women, as it were, 'the people'. Out of this amorphous Chorus, members 'crystallise out' from time to time and become recognisable to the audience as familiar characters in the Nativity Story. It is the meaning of the whole play. An actor who at one moment has been, with the others, expressing the sorrows, fears and hopes of ordinary people – the audience, ourselves – is the next moment an actor in the Mystery Play that lies at the centre of all human life: Christ is with us, of us, among us. The Nativity is seen not as an event that took place in time far away and long ago but as an event that is taking place here, now and always:

What we shall show
Is not the legend of something that once occurred
In a distant past and is gone and is done,
But a story that happens to us and to you and today
That happens to us and to you in the blood,
in the bone, in the brain,
That happens to you and through you;
that happened, and happens again.

Thus the Chorus. Then strikes in the great prose of the Bible:

"In the beginning was the Word, and the Word was with God, and the Word was God. The same was in the beginning with God".

So throughout the play, the story of the Nativity is told in the words of the English Bible projected through the texture of modern poetry, and related always to ourselves in the world today.

No more truly religious play was ever performed by the Adelphi Players than this, in spite of the exception taken by some Clergy to the 'heretical' implications of some passages in the original version, I know of no other Nativity Play, Medieval or Modern, which brings the story to the audience with more force, more immediacy, and less deadening conventionality, less sentimentality (there is not a grain of this) or less ecclesiasticism. Yet the play is liturgical in character, it has its confession, its Te Deum, its Litany. It is an organic fusion of ritual and drama, drawing its audience, as living ritual and drama must, right into itself. *Holy Family* is thus at once a great drama and a great ritual of 'The Theatre of Persons': a ritual of Art and Religion, a Christian Ritual of Persons. Some performances of *Holy Family* did justify the Company in their belief that occasionally in the course of their work, they were creating a new kind of Theatre.

Holy Family was the first, and in many ways the best, of the *Odd Plays* to which Ward referred. Its success proved that 'The Theatre of Persons' was not merely a new way of approaching existing plays, but was fruitful ground for new creative writing. So we must understand Ward's category of 'Odd' in a special sense: by it was not meant not any odd, unusual or experimental plays, but plays odd only in that they were written for actors whose ideas, circumstances of work, and theatrical values were 'odd' to most people.

The Actors are at Hand was opened at Langham, a week after *Holy Family*. It was a medley designed to supply the perennial need for a lighter and more secular Christmas show than a Nativity Play.

Next came *Brother Sin*, then some of Blake's *Songs of Innocence* and some seventeenth-century poems. Last, in the first half, Chekhov's *The Proposal*. The second half of the programme, however, fulfilled the promise implied in the Shakespearean quotation used as a title. Ward wanted, indeed felt bound by its nature and purpose, to try as soon as possible to apply the methods it was painfully hammering out of its own intractable raw material to the plays of Shakespeare. When, later, Ward conceived the idea of winding the Company up in order to create another out of its ashes, the Phoenix he envisaged was one to play Shakespeare. What he said on this occasion is worth quoting in full:

> If we attack the plays of Shakespeare we shall be trying something which is in many ways far harder than anything else we have done. God knows we must be properly humble before them. But they on their side will give far more to us actors than the plays we have been doing . . . My own inclination is to try, with the help of a little research and of such men as Granville-Barker and William Poel, to present Shakespeare as nearly as possible in the way that he was presented in his own day. The circumstances in which we work demand this simplicity, so does our own inclination and pour own revolt from the methods of contemporary Shakespeare productions . . . Our job will be to present, not ourselves in fine clothes and mouthing fine speeches, but the play – the play on a naked stage, with a minimum of trimmings and properties, with all its amazing humanity and insight, all its vision of heaven and hell, all its poetry and humour and morality laid bare. Our job is to give the play its chance to tell an audience what Shakespeare knew about the human persons who compose audiences. There never were such plays
> · as Shakespeare's for the Theatre of Persons . . . We have been unconsciously . . . fitting ourselves for a return to Shakespeare's own methods of playing and staging . . . We may be able to do all over the country and for all sorts of audiences what ventures like the Elizabethan Stage Society, at the end of the last century and the beginning of this, could only do once or twice a year and for only a select and – for the most part – 'Highbrow' few.

It is irrelevant that this Shakespeare Company never came into being. [Ward's] statement shows clearly the value placed on Shakespeare by the Company, and also what, in all humility, they felt the value of the Company could be to Shakespeare and his audience.

The second half of the programme therefore represents another important beginning – the Company's first Shakespeare. What was attempted there was modest enough. The excerpts consisted of: *Hamlet*, Act II Scene iv (the 'Closet Scene'); some of the Sonnets; *Romeo and Juliet* Act II, Scene V and Act III Scene II; and the 'Clown Scenes' from *A Midsummer Night's Dream* were a positive achievement. I would still like to have seen Ward play Hamlet, for I have seen no other Hamlet bring to the Closet scene such a bitter flame as he did.

The last of the initial group of six productions was Strindberg's *Easter*, really the first of the 'Intimate' plays.

The aim of presenting 'persons to persons' implied that the players wanted to abolish many of the differences between those **in** the play and those hearing and watching the play. The methods they used were to some extent forced on the Company by the circumstances in which they worked and (through a fortunate harmony of theory and practice) to some extent arose out of their very conception of theatre. Thus the necessity of playing to small audiences in small buildings was translated into a positive benefit to the play and those who came to see it.

The Adelphi Players realised that the small 'theatre' especially if it were in fact not constructed as a theatre, but as a bare room, or even an Air Raid Shelter, provided opportunities that the usual theatre – with its large audience firmly distanced from the actors – could not provide.

The Intimate Play, the *Kammerspiel*, the Chamber Music of the theatre, therefore had a natural attraction for the Adelphi. Of such plays, *Easter* is an excellent example, its manner being absurd, its effects subtle, its 'humanity restrained and domestic, its allegory gentle and unobtrusive. Spring was approaching too, and a Company that relied upon much of its good-will among religious bodies was glad to have a seasonable play to offer at Easter. With its several levels of meaning, its religious symbolism and its tenuous yet profound strain of mysticism, this was, indeed, a play to conjure with in 'The Theatre of Persons'.

The remaining plays of the Company's first phase may be passed over more rapidly. The next production was designed to use in churches and was a translation of a play from the old Cornish Cycles, *The Ordinalia*, and was called *The Three Maries*. A Resurrection play, it told the story of the visit of the Three Maries to the tomb on Easter morning. It was probably a descendent of that first liturgical 'drama' known as *The Quem Quaritis Trope*. The Angels moved in unison down the Chancel and the Maries circled below the chancel steps singing their sad little refrain, for which Phoebe Waterfield had made up a little plain-song-like melody. Once, at St Martin's, Bull Ring, Birmingham, the organist extemporised on this and later enquired its medieval origin! [Editor's Note: Please refer to Appendix B for a copy of the music for this refrain.]

The coming of summer, the 'Holidays at Home' policy with entertainments in public parks, demanded an open-air play. Ward's choice was Milton's *Comus*, in some ways a surprising choice for the Company's repertory. Its formal beauty and elaborate diction made demands that no previous production had made. Studied movement, broad enough to be projected over large open spaces, and a more declamatory style of speech were called for. *Comus* also had that quality of the 'allegorical' which Ward regarded as so vital.

The following Autumn and Winter found the Adelphi Players producing Flecker's *Don Juan*,[2] Susan Glaspell's *Bernice*,[3] Ward's *Mrs Henley,* and reviving *Holy Family* and *The Three Maries. Don Juan* both followed the now established traditions of the Company, and broke new ground. Flecker's character is a reincarnation of the traditional figure of the play's title. The character is primarily an idealist unable to adjust himself to reality.

We see his shooting the Prime Minister in order to prevent a war, involving him in a contradiction between ends and means which eventually destroys him, through the traditional machinery of the State. In choosing a play which thus treated problems of ends and means, of idealism, war and violence, the Company was continuing to fulfil its aim of seeking to speak to the condition of contemporary men and women. In choosing a play that had been originally refused by commercial managements, the Company emphasised their own non-commercial nature.

Bernice marked another step along the road of the deliberately intimate play. Written in the naturalistic convention by a playwright who was also a poet, it was a link between *Easter* and those later productions which were, perhaps, the peak of Adelphi work: *The Sulky Fire,* and *Ghosts.*

That detailed acting, where the slightest nuance of feeling or expression could make its effect in the small auditorium – naturalistic in an inner, not superficial, sense – provided the Adelphi with new opportunities of development.

Similar, though slighter, was *Mrs Henley,* produced because the business management wanted, or thought they wanted, a one-act play, but in fact only performed twice.

Spring 1943 marked a big break in the Repertory. As the Spring season ended, during April, each play in turn received its final performance. After a holiday the Company tackled a long and arduous rehearsal schedule. Three plays were produced, each of which holds special interest in relation to Adelphi work and history: Ibsen's *Ghosts,* Ward's *Heroic Legend of Robin Hood,* and Webster's *The Duchess of Malfi.*

It was primarily the persons in Ibsen's plays that attracted the Adelphi Players. Shaw had claimed that Ibsen was greater than Shakespeare because, while Shakespeare had shown us ourselves, Ibsen showed us ourselves in our own circumstances. Once produced, *Ghosts* became an Adelphi

---

2. *Don Juan* was written in 1910–11 by the English poet and verse dramatist James Elroy Flecker (1884–1915). Prior to the Adelphi production, it had only had a private production by the Three Hundred Club, a Sunday play-producing society which amalgamated with the Stage Society in 1924.

3. *Bernice* was written in 1919 by Susan Glaspell (1882–1948) an American dramatist, who, along with her husband George Cook and Eugene O'Neill (1888–1953), founded the Provincetown Players who were to have a decisive influence in the development of non-commercial theatre in the United States of America. This play is also of some particular interest in that it uses the device of an off-stage female protagonist.

institution. It remained in the repertory (of the First Company) for two years (May 1943 – May 1945, and then, after about fifteen months, was revived and remained until it actually inaugurated the Adelphi Guild Theatre in Macclesfield. More than any other play, it proved to the Adelphi the value of the true repertory system. The quality that drew the Adelphi to Ibsen was the depth, detail, and penetration – the truth, in a word – of his presentation of persons. To actors, therefore, who sought to express the inner truth of persons, *Ghosts* provided wonderful material that proved, as the years passed, virtually inexhaustible.

Everybody does *Ghosts*, or so we are told. Nobody, apart from the Adelphi Players, had done – or is likely to do – *The Heroic Legend of Robin Hood*. It is not a very good play but is interesting to anyone who wishes to understand the kinds of situation that arise in such a company as the Adelphi.

In outline, the play is very simple. It is Robin Hood's play about Robin – as he will appear to future generations. The slight framework of this play embodied a number of serious themes. The problem of ends and means, of doing evil that good may come inherent in the Robin Hood legend – was aired. So too was the related ethic of battle. Running through the play also is a theme of criticism of the then contemporary, orthodox theatre, in contrast with Ward's proposed Theatre of Persons.

Even more deeply woven into the play's fabric was the theme of the problems involved in the very nature of a 'Tribal' band such as that of the Outlaws and such as I have suggested the original Adelphi Company to have been. Problems of the relationship of the 'visionary' leader to his followers, of 'general' affection within the group to 'particular' affection between members of it, of the motives that draw people into such a group, and of the relationship between the fulfilment of individual capacities and that of the group's purposes are all evident.

Of much of this Ward was, of course, aware. He had seen for some time that the kinds of tensions inherent in a 'tribal' body were developing in the Company and, as an artist, he was deeply interested in them. He expected, mistakenly as events proved, that his fellow Adelphi would view the play – and its implications for them – in a similar objective light. Although rehearsals for the play went forward, they did so with growing tension, and criticism of the play on artistic grounds seems to have covered more personal and painful reactions. It was, ultimately, a trivial spark that fired the mine eventually: the flat refusal of an actor to speak a line whose good taste he questioned. However, it was enough to bring into the open the situation which had been developing and the rift between the leader and the majority of the Company was made manifest. All this was, inevitably, accompanied by a great deal of personal pain for all involved.

Meanwhile the intervention of Maurice Browne provided a temporary respite, albeit a most uncomfortable one, during which the artistic and social differences could be disentangled from the personal tensions and the new two-company system devised, as outlined previously.

The major significance of *The Duchess of Malfi* in Adelphi history is that it was the first Maurice Browne production, and his producing hand was to dominate the artistic work of the First Company for years – in some ways to the end. It was not, of course, a play to please everyone. The most revealing comment appears in a leading article in the Doncaster Gazette under the headline 'We're Ashamed'. Commenting on the lack of support in Doncaster for cultural events in connection with the wartime 'Holidays at Home' scheme, the leader writer laments that insultingly small audiences attended professional productions of A. A. Milne's *Michael and Mary*. 'Doncaster's failure to appreciate this splendid play is clear evidence of a lack of culture'. He then goes on: 'Of a different character was the play *The Duchess of Malfi* presented . . . by the Adelphi Players . . . One does not blame the average family of home-holiday makers for avoiding [this play], an Elizabethan tragedy that might possibly interest the keen student of drama but would certainly pass over the heads of ordinary people'.

Repertoire: The Second Company

There were a number of narrowly limiting factors which determined play choice in the Second Company: its size – two actors and one actress (a stage manager was also engaged) its lack of finances, and it travelled with the very minimum of properties and set in order to reach 'remote districts'.

The Second Company toured a series of productions which, taken together, represent a rather bolder and more original policy than that of the original Company. There must be few plays of quality, suitable for audiences in remote districts, capable of the simplest staging, and requiring a cast of two men and one woman. If the plays did not exist, then they must be written, and with Richard Ward involved, this was a reliable possibility. Subsequently, of the four productions toured between November 1943 and the Spring of 1945, when the Company was enlarged, three were new plays by Ward.

In addition to the limiting factors already specified, the booking of each tour added others. For example, many of the Adelphi contracts were with churches, and often in remote villages the church is the best, if not the only, place of public assembly. So we find that each play was written not only in conformity with the general requirements and limitations of the Company's work, but also to meet in each case a specific need: one is a 'church play', one a 'village hall play' and one a 'playable anywhere' play.

The first was the 'church play', *The Destiny of Man*. This was a successor to *Holy Family* and was similarly constructed. It required three actors: the protagonist, Man, and two Choruses, one male and one female. The Choruses are used, as in *Holy Family* to provide a framework of comments and to assume the parts of those with whom Man plays the crucial scenes of his life – father, mother, wife, mistress, employee, friend – and also to externalise internal dialogues between the tempter and conscience of man.

In his *Note on the plays of R H Ward*, Maurice Browne says that in *Holy Family* and the *Destiny of Man*:

> Mr Ward has, I have no doubt, made the most impressive new contribution to dramatic structure, made by any English-writing dramatist since Elizabethan times. I do not say that these two plays are necessarily great plays . . . but I do emphatically say that they show a new concept of dramatic form . . . How far the trail which Ward has blazed will be developed and widened by others, no-one, least of all its pioneer, can tell.[4]

What did this contribution to dramatic structure consist of? The key lies in having some person upon the stage who may assume at any point in the play any character which may be required at that point. This is quite different from the practice of 'doubling' for when that is done, the actor and producer do all they can to avoid the audience's being conscious of the 'double'. In the two plays under consideration, members of choruses, normally impersonal, are personalised into various characters in the course of the play without any outward changes and without leaving the stage. This not leaving the stage is essential to the way in which the structure of the play impinges on the audience. It leads, firstly, to a continuity. Not only are we free of the front curtain, of scene changes, costume changes, make up changes and similar obvious breaks in continuity, but even from that sense of a change of 'scene' that every entrance or exit provides. Only as the play can exercise a continuous hold over the audience can the dramatic tension and the great climaxes of the theatrical experience be built up.

The Choruses begin *The Destiny of Man* by saying:

> You who watch shall see exposed before you,
> Like that which is cast on a screen,
> An ordinary life. It is your own:
> For men are all one flesh and hold in common
> Breath, being, fate and destiny.

The play does emphasise too, and the Chorus points out at once, differences between individual and individual, but the whole structure implies a statement about the relationship between the individual and his fellows that could not be made theatrically in any other way. The cast is felt as a whole to be moving through a continuum of action and experience. The temporary

---

4.   As I have already noted at [1], Ward's writing deserves further discussion and evaluation. Certainly, Browne's view did not constitute the sole response to *Holy Family*. Whilst a number of reviewers commented on the qualities of the play in performance, there were, inevitably, less-favourable responses. One reviewer of the published text of the play stated: "Religious, statuesque and sincere, but lacking in freedom and spontaneity, the words do not suggest action, they do not set . . . [us] among people and events moving to a climax."

individualisations give form, pattern, highlight and shadow to the continuum, but never does one break off and assert its completely separate life. *The Destiny of Man*, 'put into new words and dresses things so deeply rooted in nature and history, that we pass them by as too familiar to notice'. Like *Holy Family* it related contemporary life, complete with air raids and war-profiteers, to fundamental religious truth. It was a play about 'essentials and the persons in whom they are vested'.

Ward also wrote a new Faust play: *Faust in Hell*. 'Faust is part of ourselves', wrote Ward in a Note to his play. He subtitled the play 'a melodrama', remarking:

> A melodrama is a stage-play having sensational incident, a strong appeal to the emotions and a happy ending . . . It should perhaps be remembered that incident is not necessarily physical, but may be psychological or spiritual, that a true appeal to the emotions is effected by sincere playing, not by 'tearing a passion to tatters'

The play, the author said, was meant to be regarded as 'contemporary' and he said it might be played in modern dress. The actual shape of the play followed very closely indeed the abbreviated version of Marlowe's play used by the original Company. The third of Ward's plays to be performed by the Second Company broke yet fresh ground. *Flora Whiteley* was, as he called it, a 'playable anywhere play'. A note from the programme of this production states:

> In this play an actress, in conversation with a young colleague, tells the story of her life . . . And because she is an actress who has spent most of life acting in the plays of Shakespeare, she uses scenes from these plays as illustrations to her narrative . . .

Unsatisfactory stage conditions – small stages, lacking curtains drapes and the like, cluttered with pianos and someone else's scenery – these had always been one of the major problems with which the Adelphi coped. Why not then, write a play whose locale is an unprepared stage? A play that actually needs a small, cluttered stage and such lighting as can be supplied by a 15 amp power point?

---

5. The Century Theatre: the naming of the fictional company in Ward's play prefigured the actual name of the unique touring theatre that he –ss along with Wilfred Harrison and the engineer John Ridley – were to envisage and build. The Century Theatre was perhaps, the final expression of the tradition of touring theatre, in that it was a theatre that, quite literally, toured theatre-less communities from the early nineteen-fifties onwards. The Century travelled Britain like a caravanserai, its company members carrying on the Adelphi values and principles of sharing all tasks and being paid equal salaries. Having moved to a static site in Keswick in Lake District, the old theatre was taken to Snibston Discovery Park near Hinckley in Leicestershire in 1997. It will continue to be a focal exhibit and educational/performance facility for the study of British touring theatre.

The cast consists of three members of an imaginary touring company, prophetically called 'The Century Shakespeare Company'.[5] In each scene Flora, as well as being the Shakespearean character: Anne, Juliet, Imogen, Desdemona, is also herself. Charles, the young actor character, as well as being Crookback, Romeo, Iachimo or Othello, is also one of Flora's husbands. Thus the structure of play is a modification of the *Holy Family* and *Destiny of Man* technique by which one person in one play plays many parts.

Not only did *Flora Whiteley* provide a full-length play for a tiny company, suitable for staging in village halls yet satisfying their desire to present Shakespeare to remote districts, but it was a further example of the creation of a dramatic form precisely appropriate to its content.

The third production of the Second Company was a double-bill: Wilfred Gibson's stark. verse-tragedy *Kestrel Edge* with the supporting play J. M. Morton's *Box and Cox*.[6] I would not hold up *Kestrel Edge* as a masterpiece. Lewis Casson, who produced, thought well of it, however, an opinion worth noting. What, perhaps, adds to the depth of this play, and helps to keep it free from the twin errors of melodrama and sentimentality, is the fact that in it no issue is clear: evil from the past clouds every issue and for no character is there a simple choice of good and evil.

Box and Cox, the supporting play in the bill, is too well known to require much comment.

The four plays planned for the International Season in 1945 were: *Faust in Hell*, *The Unknown Warrior* (Paul Raynal), *Squaring the Circle* (Kataev)[7] and Strindberg's *The Dance of Death*. *Squaring the Circle* was one of the least fortunate choices of play made in Adelphi history. Although the play is a satire on post-revolutionary Russia, originally intended for internal consumption, we felt that it should have a wide appeal. However, audiences did not find it so, and the reason may have lain in the production.

The other new play in the repertory, *The Unknown Warrior* was the only play that was included in the repertories of both the First and Second Companies. This was one of the greatest plays to be performed by the Companies, and while it undoubtedly did poor box office, impressed those who saw it very deeply. It was published in France in 1924. Four years earlier, it had been 'his first play to be performed and had established him as a dramatist of the first importance.' Four years later again, in 1928, it was produced under translated title as *The Unknown Warrior* at The Cambridge Arts Theatre, with Maurice Browne as The Soldier.

---

6.   *Box and Cox* a popular and, at one time, frequently-produced one act farce (1847) written by John Maddison Morton (1811–91).

7.   *Squaring the Circle* (1928) was by far the most successful play of the Russian dramatist Valentin Petrovich Katayev (1897–1986). It was first produced at the Moscow Arts Theatre, seen in New York in 1935, and in London in 1938. It is a comedy of two couples who, due to a housing shortage, are forced to share accomodation and, eventually, exchange partners.

The Second Company ended its existence presenting this play in the New Lindsey Theatre at Notting Hill Gate, and it could scarcely have ended playing a better play to smaller audiences.

Certain features in the First Company's repertory mark it off clearly from that of the original Company. The 'production rate' was lower. The plays were usually carried for many months, and whereas the original Adelphi Players had produced fourteen plays (excluding revivals) in a period of two years and four months, the First Company produced only nine (excluding revivals and *Ghosts*, a heritage of the original Adelphi Players). Before considering the implications of this, we must notice the other features. Of these nine plays only one, *Shadow and Substance*, had 'religious' subject matter, and not one was a 'religious' play in the stricter sense. Of the fourteen plays of the original Adelphi Players, four had been 'religious' by definition, and two others, *Dr Faustus* and *Comus*, were 'borderline cases'. Thus another feature of the First Company's repertory was that it was, in a popular sense, more 'secular' than that of the original Adelphi Players.

Next, we observe that of the original fourteen plays, two were brand new, two: *Don Juan* and *Mrs Henley*, had only once been professionally produced before, and of the remainder, one was a new version, one an original mixture, and one – *The Three Maries* – a rarity. First Company's nine on the other hand, only one was a first production, and that only of a new translation: *The Bachelor*. Of the remainder only Raynal's *Unknown Warrior* was a really unusual play, though Singe's *Dierdre* is perhaps rarely done in England. These changes in emphasis are considerable and mark a real change in policy, partly conscious, partly unconscious. The smaller numbers of productions arose from policy. One of the points of difference between the First and Second Companies lay in the emphasis which the former placed on artistic development in the narrower sense. This tendency was greatly accentuated by the influence of Maurice Browne who, it would appear, had little sympathy with most of the social ideals of the Company, but who realised at once its artistic potentialities. He became, in effect, the First Company's producer.

Also, once a production was in the repertory, the Company naturally wished to make the fullest possible use of it. They found furthermore, that as one play was never performed exclusively, a relatively long 'run' allowed valuable opportunities for the deepening and enriching of performances, and of the integration of all aspects of production in artistic unity.

This preoccupation with production tended to lead to a slightly changed attitude to the choice of plays. At first, perhaps, it was not very marked. Observe that the one 'new' play was its second production.

It would be unfair to the Company to suggest that it deliberately avoided the new, the contemporary or the unknown. Indeed, its members were acutely conscious that a theatrical movement that did not give birth to its own dramatist or dramatists was doomed in the end to failure. It was apparently their anxiety to maintain 'high artistic standards' made them chary of new plays. Even Turgenev's *The Bachelor* gave rise to numerous debates and was nearly dropped after being produced. How many new plays the Company turned down, I do not know, but one at least, *Prisoners,* was an extremely good play and in every way suitable for the Company's purposes; yet it was rejected: it was by R. H. Ward! Changes in the repertory's character reflected also the change of Director. In spite, therefore, of the formal appointment of certain members as readers who passed on recommendations to the Director (Browne), the responsibility rested ultimately upon him. This partly accounts for the secularisation of the repertory, for Browne had not that strong religious strain that marked Ward's character.

Apart from these general considerations there is less to be said about the plays of this phase. This phase was marked by changes in matters of production, and by the development of actors rather than by adventurousness in choice of repertory.

If the *Duchess of Malfi* marked in many ways the height of achievement of the original Adelphi Players, *The Sulky Fire* – the first production of the First Company, was in many ways the high water mark of the whole Adelphi work.[8] The play, and Bernard's style, offered the Company a most fruitful field to which to apply their ideas of intimacy, details, and inner sincerity.

This thoroughness of detail was one of Browne's chief contributions to the work. The play itself was right in the mainstream of Adelphi tradition, and its Great War situation very topical in the World War. Delicacy of touch was manifested also in Turgenev's charming comedy *The Bachelor*, in which the trivialities of conversation are employed to reveal deeper feelings. Other plays of this phase will be better discussed in a later chapter.

The next phase was the Cornish Season of 1946. Naturally, a number of plays were needed to put the plan into practice, and the old scheme of non-playing rehearsal periods was dropped. Instead, plays were rehearsed at Camborne and the Company would then set out in the evening to perform something already in the Repertory. The season began with *Shadow and Substance*[9] and *An Enemy of the People*, already in stock. During the summer were added *Arms and the Man*, *Mr Bolfry*, *The Unknown Warrior* and a revival of *Ghosts*. This group of plays chosen for what was, in effect, a 'resident' season, reveals a new factor in the choice of plays – a desire for 'balance'. A Company touring indiscriminately, frequently visiting places served also by

---

8. *The Sulky Fire* (1921, translated into English, 1926) is a moving play written by Jean-Jacques Bernard (1888–1972) whose work was influenced by the *Ecole Intimiste* (Theatre of Silence) of Maeterlinck (1862–1949). In terms of what Cecil Davies describes as the understated performance style sought by the Adelphi, it is no surprise that Bernard's writing was both so appropriate for – and popular with – the Company. The Theatre of Silence was characterised by a dialogue of economy and of the 'silent' sub-text underlying the dramatic action. Bernard's plays were several times revived at both the Cambridge Arts Theatre and the Gate Theatre up until 1949.
9. *Shadow and Substance* (1934): was probably the best known, and best play, by the Irish dramatist Paul Vincent Carroll (1900–68). It received an award as Best Foreign Play of 1938 in New York and was first seen in London in 1943.

other companies, had no need to worry about this. However, a five month season in a limited area made new demands and in two ways. From the business point of view, it seemed necessary to provide a repertory in which some plays might appeal to members of the public who would not care for others. To include some plays of greater popular appeal than most of those of earlier days was felt to be not only legitimate but a duty, for the towns visited that Summer were almost entirely dependent upon the Adelphi Season for their theatrical entertainment.

This did not prevent the inclusion of a play of such severity as *The Unknown Warrior* but it led to the inclusion of *Arms and the Man* and *Mr Bolfry*. During the following Autumn the similar season based on Stoke-on-Trent used some of the same repertory with the addition of a revival (virtually a new production) of *Twelfth Night*. However when in the early months of 1947, the Company settled in Macclesfield, the intention to serve a limited number of towns arranged in a monthly or five-weekly cycle, became of the greatest importance in determining repertory. The Company now definitely regarded its function as having changed. Within the Arts Council system of regionalised touring companies, working from suitable bases, it was to be – for many places within travelling distance of Macclesfield – **the** theatre. From this time the plays seemed to fall roughly into two classes: those the Adelphi Guild did not object to doing, and those they really wanted to do. A real problem is raised here to which no rigid solution can be offered. Was it right or wrong for the Company to deviate from its old way of choosing plays in view of the new situation?

By the time the Adelphi settled in Macclesfield and became the Adelphi Guild Theatre, members wanted many things, and to different degrees. Some wanted to establish a theatre rooted in community, some to produce plays such as they had produced in the past. Others sought to combine the theatre with a tolerable married life, whilst yet others were committed to develop their own acting and broader staging methods. It was imagined that unity could be maintained on the basis of the common approach to the problems of acting and production, but one year was to prove that this was an inadequate foundation. Although during this period of disintegration much of value was to be done, the work began to lose the special flavour that had till then justified the Company's existence.

The new phase was linked to the old by *Ghosts* which had not been performed in Macclesfield or in several of the places near. This was followed

---

10. *Thunder Rock* (1939) is an extremely interesting example of plays chosen for the Adelphi repertoire. An allegorical anti-war play by the American dramatist Robert Ardrey, the first London production opened at a 'fringe' theatre called The Neighbourhood, in Kensington before transferring to the Globe Theatre. Clearly, the play's anti-militaristic themes and its evident contemporary popularity, indicate the extent to which the Adelphi were prepared to select plays which were both contemporary, and in keeping with the broader ethical and ideological background of the Company.

by Priestley's *I Have Been Here Before*, a play which might conceivably have been included in earlier repertories, but would *The Duke in Darkness* and *Thunder Rock*.[10] The remaining play of this season belonged more clearly to the 'Adelphi heritage'. *The Moon in the Yellow River* had all the qualities one associates with the Adelphi's work. While it was well liked by audiences, it was not chosen, as to some extent the others were, with the imagined needs of the audience in mind.[11]

After a financially disastrous Summer Season in Northern Ireland, the second Winter based on Macclesfield was begun with James Bridie's *It Depends What You Mean*. It was probably one of the slightest plays that the Adelphis had ever chosen. Its inclusion on grounds of mere innocuousness was an unfortunate precedent.

Dissatisfaction and a growing lack of trust between Company and Director marked the time that followed.

Toad of Toad Hall – the 1947 Christmas Play – was one of the happiest of all Adelphi productions. In the Spring, *Eden End*, *She Stoops to Conquer* and *The Wise Have Not Spoken* seemed at the time to be leading to a Renaissance. But the Director and the Company had been, evidently, at cross-purposes. The repertory of the 1948–9 season was, on the whole, almost as unlike the general body of Adelphi work as the majority of the persons employed (the 'Crazy Gang', as they were nicknamed by some of the dispossessed players) were unlike the majority of Adelphi personnel. Even the fact that Ward produced *An Inspector Calls* and *The Whole World Over* by Konstantin Simonov and Thelma Schnee was interesting enough, the trend away from original ideals seemed remorseless. The inclusion of *The Simpleton of the Unexpected Isles* showed fairly conclusively that the Adelphi Guild Theatre no longer had the aims of Richard Ward's 'Theatre of Persons'.[12]

---

11. Denis Johnston's (1901–1934) *The Moon in the Yellow River* (1931) was one of the author's more successful Symbolist-genre plays. Many of this Irish dramatist's plays were produced at the Gate Theatre in Dublin, of which he was joint manager.

12. Cecil Davies' observation about the 'trend away from original ideals' requires some consideration in terms of the Adelphi Guild Theatre's repertoire. Certainly, the inclusion of Vincent Carroll's *The Wise Have Not Spoken* (1933, London 1946) reflects, as Davies suggests, a possible 'renaissance' for the Company at that period. Equally, *The Whole World Over* by Konstantin Simonov (1915–79), a Russian dramatist whose reputation was well established by this time, seems quite progressive in tone. Nevertheless, these sit uncomfortably, perhaps, with a lesser and lightweight play: *The Simpleton of the Unexpected Isles* (1935), albeit by an author of Shaw's (1856–1950) reputation. With critical and objective hindsight, it must be argued that the Company had always – as all companies touring under such circumstances must – mixed the progressive with the 'standard fare' of contemporary repertory theatre. For example, even the original Adelphi Players had been obliged to produce 'lightweight' Housman with Strindberg and Glaspell. It is probable too that Ward himself recognised the pragmatic need for plays that were more likely to attract audiences, alongside those that were challenging in their themes and style. Ultimately, the fact that writers like Bernard, Carroll and Glaspell were featuring in the Adelphi repertoire at all (when their London productions were often at non-commercial theatres such as The Gate) is an incontrovertible indication of their commitment, where possible, to progressive programming.

The timing of the Annual General Meeting did not coincide with the ending of the season, with the result that when the majority of the legal membership regained working control of the Company, there was still one more play to be chosen, rehearsed and performed before the Summer break. The choice of Bridie's *Tobias and the Angel* is interesting, for it is a play belonging in a number of ways to the original Adelphi tradition. It was the first play on a strictly religious theme since the Adelphi Guild Theatre had made Macclesfield their centre. It was a Pilgrims Players play. It was unpretentious and fundamentally simple. The production had to cost very little, but one's impression was of deliberate and artistically successful simplicity, not of involuntary economy.

After the Summer break, the reformed company had to try to express its nature in terms of a repertory season. This was inevitably a period of increasing economic difficulties. *The Hasty Heart* served well to open the season, whilst Somerset Maugham's *Sheppey* followed. *Alice in Wonderland* followed as the Christmas production whilst the New Year opened with *Dandy Dick*. Interestingly, a new play by a local author, Leonard Irwin followed; *Land of the Living*. It was not well received by the newspaper critics, whose major comments were based on the general argument that the characters were stock types. In order to decide on the closing production of the 1949–50 Season, the Adelphi Guild Theatre instituted a public poll by which a number of plays were 'nominated' and then voted for by their audiences. The 'winner' was *Macbeth*. The ex-Adelphi, Wilfred Harrison was brought in to play the title role, whilst Richard Ward was brought back as producer. Phoebe Waterfield also 'returned' to play Lady Macbeth. Thus, quite naturally, *Macbeth* became a joint production of the Adelphi Guild Theatre and the embryonic Century Theatre. The designs were made by T. Osborne Robinson of the Northampton Repertory Company, who had designed for the Adelphi as far back as *Comus*. In 1942 while the Witches' masks were made by John Crockett, thus relating the Compass Players to this production as well.[13] The successful production of *Macbeth* was the late full blossoming of the life and spirit of the Adelphi.

The last, incomplete Season of the Adelphi Guild Theatre's existence was bedevilled by small houses, rising costs, blunted by aims divided,

---

13. John Crockett (1918–86) was the founder, in 1944, of the Compass Players who were yet another company committed both to community living and touring broadly progressive, innovative theatre to theatre-less communities. Crockett was a very fine painter and had also attended classes at the London Theatre Studio, founded and run by Michel Saint-Denis (1897–1971) and George Devine (1910–65). At Goldsmiths College, Crockett studied Theatre Design under Polunin who had worked in collaboration with Picasso and Leger in designs for Diaghilev. Osborne Robinson was a very highly-respected theatre designer for over three decades. He worked principally for Northampton Royal Repertory Theatre, where he had arrived as resident designer in 1928. Robinson worked as a Guest Designer on several Adelphi productions, perhaps most notably the open-air 1942 production of Milton's *Comus*.

understandably, between artistic integrity and solvency. It was also a Season marked up to the last by courage, enterprise and principle.

The plays were: *The Bubble* by Leonard Irwin, *Mr Gillie* by James Bridie, *The Rose and the Ring* by Thackeray, *The Prince of Darkness is a Gentleman* by Cecil Davies and, finally, *Prophesy to the Wind* by Norman Nicholson.

After a brief visit to Northern Ireland with *Mr Gillie*, the Adelphi Guild Theatre returned with the first play by an Adelphi Company member since *Robin Hood*. A critique of this play is impossible in this book, it could only be a confiteor.

The play concerns the dilemma of a liberal idealist engaged in educational work who finds that his friend and colleague, an avowed Communist, is unscrupulously manipulating the policy of the Association for which they both work. Written in 1948 before McCarthy had become a name with which to conjure up the devils of intolerance, the play suggested that this dilemma might well be more real than liberal democrats liked to believe.

The provocation which the play evoked in critics and audiences was sometimes almost too great and caused embarrassment to the author and friends. Inevitably, several groups of people felt that they had been both represented and misrepresented, and at one point there was even the rumour of legal action. This never materialised.

1951 had begun. It was ten years since the original Company had been brought together by Richard Ward. Of its members, there remained only Molly Sole, John Headley and Piers Plowman (who had joined in 1942). The programme note of the final production stated:

> What is the proper function of a theatre company such as ours? First and foremost it must surely be to entertain. But there are ways and means of entertaining, and a potent form which suffers too much neglect is the performing of new plays which have a particular concern with the values and perils of contemporary life. A new play is a risk to put on and the cost of a production is a heavy item in our budget. But a group of people who do not take risks for what they believe to be worth-while, and hence enjoyable, is surely doomed to failure.

This last statement of policy for the professional premiere of Norman Nicholson's *Prophesy to the Wind* had brave words in it, though the Company also knew that those who do take risks for their beliefs may, also, fail. The Adelphi Guild Theatre had chosen for Festival Play in Festival of Britain Year, a play about the future. Its theme: that in spite of his failures, his stupidity, his moral blindness, his crude brutality, Man will always move out of death to a new resurrection, was itself an apt comment on a play whose very run was to be curtailed by the liquidation of the Company.[14]

The 'kitty' was empty, and a Company without money cannot continue its corporate existence. Relatively few saw this play before the Adelphi Guild Theatre died.

But even as the Adelphi years came to a sad end, the Compass Players were still working, and in the inauspicious setting of the Water Works Yard at Hinckley, Leicestershire, the fabric of the Century Theatre was slowly taking shape ...

14. Norman Nicholson's *Prophesy to the Wind* was yet another example of the Cumbrian poet's experiments with religious verse drama. Its inclusion in the Adelphi Guild's final repertoire would have carried a particularly progressive, experimental resonance in that period. This reflected the ongoing interest in, and development of, verse – or poetic – drama. It should be remembered that Eliot's *The Cocktail Party* had been premiered as recently as 1949 at the inaugural Edinburgh Festival. This premiere had been produced by Elliott Martin Browne, founder of the Pilgrim Players and occasional director with the Adelphi. In 1945, Browne produced a season of new religious verse plays at the Mercury Theatre which he had leased from Ashley Dukes, its owner. There was early critical success with Ronald Duncan's *This Way to the Tomb*, following which Browne was able to bring two other plays into the repertoire: Nicholson's *Old Man of the Mountains* and Ann Ridler's *The Shadow Factory*. Therefore, for the Adelphi Guild to be producing Nicholson's work was, again, a clear indication of their engagement with work which was – in its genre – both new and progressive.

3

THE ACTING

The Times once referred casually to Adelphi acting [in an early performance of Housman's *Abraham and Isaac* at Westminster Cathedral Hall] as having 'sensitivity and intelligence'.[1] A primary principle of the Adelphi Players, and one which they never abandoned, was that their business was not self-display but self-abnegation. Nothing must be placed between play and audience; the best actor clearly revealed the author's meaning.

A green room story is told of trouble with a door in the set during a West End dress rehearsal. The producer called the Stage Manager out in front of the cast. "Mr Stage Manager", he said, "that door must be made fool-proof, actors have to use it".

However, intelligence alone will not result in good acting. Sensitivity is even more important, for it perceives different dimensions of meaning: those which give the script height and depth and breadth. Sensitivity is more important than intelligence in the understanding of character, in appreciating a situation, in absorbing an atmosphere. Whilst intelligence can censor the actor's performance, that cannot in the first place be created without sensitivity.

As the Adelphi aimed to present 'Persons to Persons', for this to be done the characters must be understood and felt with sensitivity and intelligence. This leads on to the approach to the script. Nothing must be done which was irrelevant to the text, or which contradicted it, or obscured it, which distorted it for some secondary end. On the other hand, the text as it came to the Company was not treated with superstitious awe.

In truth, the Adelphi asserted the play. They respected the spirit and not the letter of the author's intention, and sought never to distort it. With this attitude towards the script, the first aim of the acting was transparency, the removal of obstacles between the play and the audience of which the most obvious an actor can place are his technique and himself.

It will be recalled that Ward said that in the early stages, the development of a new technique for the 'Theatre of Persons' must take the form of the eradication of the old theatrical technique. While, in 1941, any experienced

---

1.   *Abraham and Isaac.* The following extract is taken from a review of the original Adelphi Players production of this play. The review appeared in *The Times* 25 August 1941: 'The Adelphi Players have been doing splendid work in helping top keep the theatre alive in the adverse conditions of war; it is fitting that they should give their first performance of Housman's *Abraham and Isaac* at the Westminster Cathedral Hall where their acting was sensitive and intelligent'.

actor would have pronounced bluntly and forcibly that most of the actors had no technique whatsoever, they had something that required eradication just as seriously: either bad technique or the tendency to develop the old technique. Ward and Phoebe Waterfield had training and some little experience in the 'old theatre'. Jane Fitz-Gerald and Greta Newell had also had training, [Greta Newell at the then relatively new Central School]. The remaining members at that early stage had no professional training and only amateur experience. There was, then, plenty to be 'eradicated'. I can best illustrate if I may be forgiven, from my own case and experience.

Even at best I have never been of much value to the theatre as an actor – a small part man only. The Adelphi Players did make me an actor, within my own limits. When I joined the Adelphi Players, I had a fair amount of amateur experience, I had even played one or two small parts with professionals. I also had a theoretical knowledge of Stanislavsky's ideas and methods and was ground in which the seed of the personal theatre could be planted.

How Richard Ward endured some of our performances in those first months I do not know, although he began to lead us in the right direction. In Housman's *Brother Sin*, I had a prayer – a passage in which from the beginning I had rather fancied myself. I was downstage Centre Right, I remember, and was usually lit by a floodlight with a straw-coloured 'jelly' [transparent, coloured, lighting filter] When we were preparing for a performance at the Questors Theatre, Ealing, and were using the lighting plant there, Ward told me to take up the position for the prayer. He then instructed John Headley to direct a blue spotlight on me. I of course, was rather flattered at the trouble taken to light my favourite 'set piece'. Richard Ward suddenly asked me, "Do you know why I'm having this steel blue on you for the prayer?" "No", I replied. "Because", he said harshly, and I think in rather stronger language than this, "you are making such a slush of it". It was the most salutary lesson I ever learned in the theatre. What was it that Ward, and by implication, the Adelphi Players, were so anxious to eradicate in terms of themselves and acting style? It was clearly something more than such elementary crudities as occured in my attempt to play St Francis. In this issue, as in some others, Ward and the Adelphi moved a little apart from the main stream of the theatre.

The, at that time, effete West End style of acting, designed to provide innocuous entertainment to stalls well wined and dined, would have been useless in the Air Raid Shelters of the East End, while blustering histrionics would have raised well-earned guffaws, as well as being out of place in the church chancel that was so often the Adelphi stage. The acting style they sought to develop was organic acting, growing out of an inner state of being, finding expression in restraint or heroics according to the play's demands.

Ward and the Adelphi therefore meant to eradicate the 'old' technique: something apparently complex but fundamentally simple. The orthodox theatre, whether naturalistic or Grand, the majority of Drama Schools, most theatre managers, producers and critics, laid great stress on the **externals** of technique: the production of the voice, diction, movement - all things important and essential to acting, but only as instruments and means, not as **ends** in themselves.

The Adelphi Players, on the contrary, stressed the importance of the internal, the mental and spiritual technique. As usually practised, both the 'naturalistic' and 'heroic' styles relied very largely on external qualities, so that the naturalism was superficial and the heroic merely showy. Ward saw that, as Ward and his actors also realised that external technique draws attention not only to itself at the expense of the play, but also to the actor. The audience were not to be given the opportunity of admiring technique for technique's sake.

It was, then, to Stanislavsky rather than to Coquelin,[2] that the Adelphi Players turned for inspiration and guidance.

The three great fundamentals of Stanislavaky's theories were subscribed to by the Adelphi: sincerity, concentration and consciousness. Re-creative acting which demands we live through the play in every performance searches out weakness and shallowness of motives and reactions even after rehearsals have finished; and it characteristic of Adelphi productions that they gained remarkably in depth and humanity during the time they were in stock.

Most of the training which Stanislavsky devised for his students is directed to the two simple ends of achieving real sincerity, and of allowing that inner sincerity to reach the audience.

Concentration concerned the Adelphi deeply as well. The two great obstacles to concentration are: the practical problems of the stage and the presence of the audience. How deeply the practical problems modified the acting I did not realise fully until, later, I found myself in a repertory company where I was on the same stage, day in day out, for thirty or forty weeks in the year. Only then I appreciated how much mental energy and conscious concentration had to be diverted from the play to the stage. The undertaking by the Adelphi to play anywhere where there was room for ourselves and

---

2. Constant-Benolt Coquelin (1841–1909) was a great French actor, outstanding in the great comic roles of Molière and in flamboyant modern parts. Along with his younger brother, Ernest-Alexandre, he was a leading figure at the Comédie-Française. Davies' reference to him in relation to Stanislavsky is significant in that Coquelin's approach to characterisation and performance style was characterised by an 'externalised' bravura and rhythm. The issue of the influence of Stanislavskian ideas upon Ward and, by implication, the Company, deserves more detailed discussion than can be provided in this context. Nevertheless, the Moscow Art Theatre had played *The Cherry Orchard* on a visit to London in 1928 at the Garrick Theatre. Clearly, the references that Davies makes to Stanislavskian ideas and methodology can only be partial. It might be significant that a substantial proportion of Stanislavsky's attention was devoted to the requirement that the actor should be able to enter a state of physical, muscular relaxation. This recognition of the need for a sensitively-tuned physicality has sometimes been neglected at the expense of a preoccupation with the inner, psychological aspects of the Stanislavskian System.

the audience, meant that we used almost as many spaces as we gave performances. In these circumstances there were perpetual problems modification, some decided before the performance, others improvised within it. This unfamiliarity with every stage undoubtedly limited the acting. There was, however, a credit side also to the physical conditions of the work in the early phases: limitations of a medium can stimulate an artist. The very determination not to allow a particularly awkward chair, or odd stage, to mar the performance kept the Adelphi always alert.

Within the very flexible framework that the production provided, much physical movement, business, and timing, had to be determined in the very midst of acting pattern. The Adelphi were, therefore, in little danger at that time of allowing a hollow externality to be a substitute for inner reality: the chief danger was the contrary one, that from time to time, the actor would fail to adapt himself to circumstances and the projection would be rough or weak.

The other great obstacle to concentration, the audience, also affected the Adelphi in a special way. Rarely was the audience cut off from the actors by the physical barriers of proscenium arch and powerful stage lighting. More frequently, the whole of the audience was clearly visible to them and often the nearest members of the audience were no further from the actor than were his fellow actors. The particular difficulty raised by this situation was felt especially by those actors who were conscious of the close relationship between their ideas and those of Stanislavsky. The question was raised as to whether a concept, that of forgetting the audience in order to concentrate upon the life being portrayed on the stage, which had been formulated in application to the proscenium stage, could rightly find its place in Adelphi work. Whilst attempts at answering these issues did not magically solve the problems, the special quality of the actor-audience relationship which Adelphi actors gradually developed became one of the distinguishing marks of their work. In January 1942, Ward, in discussion, answered the question by saying that the actor should not be conscious of the audience as individuals, but only as a collective audience between which and himself the actor must feel an invisible line of communication.

These particular circumstances were, of course, nothing new. Two parallels with their own situation often struck the Adelphi Players: the Elizabethan theatre and the Music Hall. The former we know only by report, but it does appear that in its circumstances of daylight and an audience as close to the Players as an Adelphi audience, great acting was possible. The study of Shakespeare and his contemporaries, such as Marlowe, can throw light in the kind of actor-audience relationship required in those physical circumstances. It seems plain that closed world of concentration is not appropriate. The great soliloquies of *Hamlet* or *Dr Faustus* call for a far closer, more conscious link between player and audience. This 'thinking aloud' in public becomes patently artificial unless the actor can, as it were, share his inner self with the audience.

The great comedians of the Music Hall stage seem to have preserved an authentic tradition of close contact with their audience. Even the rawest Music Hall comedian has the art of drawing the audience into the show, of making a direct personal contact with them: and it well to remember that **his** personality is as much a 'part' as that of the 'straight' actor. So from the Music Hall too, the Adelphi felt that they had lessons to learn, to help them work out the techniques needed to achieve the maximum reality, humanity and personalism within the play. At the same time, the artificial and comparatively modern barrier between the actor and audience – symbolised in the proscenium arch – might be broken down. Part of the problem of concentration is in the last of the three fundamental Stanislavskian concepts identified: consciousness. Not only should the actor be aware in himself of the basic 'I am I', but also that 'I am Hamlet' or whoever.

The actor only aware of the 'I am I' is, of course, no actor at all but merely someone exploiting his own personality upon the stage – an all too common phenomenon.

While the 'Hamlet' personality will concentrate on the imaginative world of the play, the 'I' personality will foresee and solve the practical problem of the stage, and adjust the relationship between the 'Hamlet' personality and the audience. Maintaining the balance of the dual personality is a basic and essential technique of the actor; but however the balance is maintained, the 'I' personality is never central.

The Adelphi realised that, however great the importance of operating the 'inner man' it was through the mediation of the 'outer man' – his voice, his appearance, his movement – that he would create his link with the audience.

The Adelphi, therefore, could not ignore the technical demands of speech and movement. They declared the necessity of eradicating the 'old technique' in the sense of the generally accepted methods of elocution and stage movement. There was some on-going debate within the Company from earliest days as to how the demands of speech and movement might be met. On the one hand, there were those, including Ward, who emphasised the dangers of actual classes. The best kind of training, according to this school of thought – which predominated as a rule – was that actual playing and experience, especially in the kinds of conditions faced by the Company – was the best training. On the other hand, it was pointed out by others that there were limits to this approach. Inability to control the body might have serious or ludicrous results. Surely it would be better, through classes, for the fault(s) to be corrected?

General agreement was usually reached in the position that knowledge of the fundamentals of speech and movement were as desirable to the actor as perspective to the artist, but that the least tendency for conscious correctness to become an end in itself was diametrically opposed to the aims of the Theatre of Persons.

Accordingly, the Company largely learnt its technique through playing. However, in November 1943, a few months after he had become Director of the First Company, Jack Boyd Brent did seriously put forward a scheme for class work and seminars. The Company were to meet every other morning for two hours. He was very anxious that the class work should be treated seriously and given the same precedence as rehearsals. He proposed four possible fields of work:

Understudy Rehearsals
Play Readings
Technical Exercises
Lectures and Debates

Usually understudying had been out of question in so small a company. An illness, if really serious, had meant cancelling a show – and hastily summoning someone to fill the gap. However, it seems clear that there was a stronger motive for them than mere provision against accident or illness. They were evidently introduced partly to provide additional training. I cannot find that the other three proposals were ever put into practice, apart from occasional readings of plays under consideration for the repertory. It may legitimately be asked what the consequences of these discussions and attempts were in actual acting and performance terms. The answers which can be offered are bound to be unsatisfactory.

Anecdotally and personally, individual moments remain impressed upon my mind which may perhaps be recalled. Vividly clear are Wilfred Harrison and Phoebe Waterfield as Macbeth and Lady Macbeth, sitting, simply sitting, crowned and in royal robes: disillusioned. There is Jack Boyd Brent as Dobell in *The Moon in the Yellow River*, playing with quiet focus with his model railway in the midst of turmoil. It may be even more appropriate to try to convey the impression made by one good, typical performance: John Headley's Engstrand from Ibsen's *Ghosts* is such a one.

Knowing how far the trade makes the man, and a joiner himself, Headley presented from the first moments of the play an Engstrand who was plainly a carpenter. His complexion was coarse-grained and ruddy not only through years of work in half-built houses, but also through 'the bottle'. His dark eyes, under thick brows, and pouched below by dissipation, looked out at one warily and resentfully when he was not observed, but were able to assume an expression of uncultured honesty when necessary. As he peered through the conservatory panes at the opening of the play, he struck the observer as at once evil and servile, contemptible and dangerous, and when he spoke, his rough accent established the character of an 'honest Iago'. Such an Engstrand struck notes of comedy, just as does Ibsen's first stage direction of Regina, with a garden syringe – empty. As Engstrand came to us partly as a comic character, he won a measure of sympathy in the face of Regina's snobbish and callous attitude to his foot and speech. As the tone of the play became, in the later acts, more sombre, so did Engstrand – appearing more – provide contrast. So excellently written is the part of Engstrand that it is possible, indeed easy, for a good, but selfish actor, to 'steal the play' with it.

John Headley did not do this either. If he avoided the grotesque and monstrous, he avoided also all superficial comedy: there was no gesture, no inflection simply designed to provoke mirth. Instead, every inflection, every movement arose out of the workings of the character, and the laughter evoked was not sharp reaction to the obviously funny, but deep response to the immensely comic. John Headley revealed Ibsen's Engstrand to be a great comic character, strong, deep, rounded and truer and, like some of Shakespeare's characters capable of living fully in a fundamentally tragic play.[3]

---

3.   The late John Headley had joined the Adelphi Players very early on in the original Company's existence, and in rather unusual circumstances. The following transcript from his recorded response to some questions that I had presented to him, is quite revealing in terms of the broader socio/cultural background of their origins:

'I was working in an Educational Settlement in the Rhondda Valley before the war in a training scheme for disabled lads. We had a visit at the beginning of the war from the Old Vic, led by Sybil Thorndike and Lewis Casson and they did *The Medea* and *Macbeth*. I spent one afternoon taking Sybil around the Rhondda Valley visiting the Unemployed Clubs ... so I began to get interested in the theatre. When Richard Ward came down with a Pilgrim production of [Bridie's] *Tobias and the Angel* in our hall, someone had got 'flu and so I had to stand in and got to know Richard. When he wanted to start his own company early in 1941, he persuaded me to come and join the Company on the basis of organising transport, making props and things like that.' [John Headley, in recorded interview, April 1990.]

2. Richard Ward's *Holy Family*, Ilkley Playhouse, April 1942. Directed by Richard Ward. Featuring, left to right (standing) Wilfred Harrison, John Headley and Jack Boyd Brent; left to right (kneeling) Piers Plowman, Greta Newell, Phoebe Waterfield and Jane Fitz-Gerald. Photographer unknown.

3. Adelphi Players preparing backstage for their production of Strindberg's *Easter*. Directed by Elliot Martin Browne, 1942. Featuring (left to right) Richard Ward and Jack Boyd Brent. Photographer unknown.

Mephistophilis & Faustus. — Marlowe's Dr Faustus. The Adelphi Players Worcester Cathedral.

4. Adelphi Players in Ward's abridged version of Marlowe's *Dr Faustus*. Open-air production at Worcester Cathedral, 12 July 1942. Directed by, and featuring (right) as Faustus, Richard Ward. Featuring (left) J. Boyd Brent as Mephistopheles. Photographer unknown.

5. The Adelphi Guild Theatre production of Robert Ardrey's *Thunder Rock*, 1947. Featuring, left to right, Bernard Rumball and Valerie Gray. Directed by Jack Boyd Brent. Design: J. B. Brent and Cecil W. Davies. Photographer: John Dodds.

6. The Adelphi Guild Theatre production of James Bridie's *It Depends What You Mean*, 1947. Directed by Jack Boyd Brent. Design: Cecil W. Davies. Featuring, left to right, Bernard Rumball, Greta Newell and Ronald Sly. Photographer: John Dodds.

7. The setting, designed by Cecil W. Davies, of the Adelphi Guild Theatre production of Paul Vincent Carroll's *The Wise Have Not Spoken*, Manchester Library Theatre, 1948. Directed by John Headley with assistance by R. H. Ward. Photographer: John Dodds

8. The Adelphi Guild Theatre production of Cecil Davies' *The Prince of Darkness is a Gentleman*, 1950. Directed by John Headley. Design Richard Jerrams and Cecil W. Davies. Featuring, from left to right, Jean Alexander, Ronald Lane and Noel Lloyd. Photographer: John Dodds

4

THE VISUAL ELEMENTS AND PRODUCTION

Earlier in this account of the Adelphi Players, I remarked that materials for the first production could be carried, unaided, to the place of performance. The costumes, all but one simple Franciscan habits, were made into individual bundles and tied with their own rope girdles so that each character carried his own. Properties were carried in a wooden box. Essential to the production were two wooden stools. That was all. This complete reliance upon whatever setting they might find appeared even in the first phase only at open air performances, in daylight. Usually, they had two simple means of adapting the setting provided:

1) A pair of two-leaf folding screens, covered with plain hessian.
2) A couple of completely plain, home-made, tin plate 'floodlights' (little more than tins without lids) together with a quantity of flex and a small collection of electric plugs and adaptors. The screens were, at first, entirely functional, being used to provide exits where none existed, to mask doors of ante-rooms, and even, on one or two memorably uncomfortable occasions, to provide a diminutive dressing room for the entire cast. In this way, the screens became part of the show seen, but only because they were a practical necessity. The first step beyond this was taken, when, at some early performance, the screens were used to hide a hideous radiator, or irrelevant picture, because it was felt that their plain neutrality was preferable as a background for the action to the object they were used to cover. Once they had been consciously preferred as a setting to something else, however hideous, the way was open for them to be thought of as a planned and desirable setting.

If tempted to think that the Adelphi Players were simply making the best of a bad job, one must remember that they had chosen to work in these conditions of simplicity and improvisation. When Ward wrote in his manifesto article "The Theatre of Persons" of the progressive theatre of the future, he stated:

> Of one thing this theatre will have to be convinced: the properness of improvisation. An art cannot be a fixed institution . . . The formed theatre must be endlessly adaptable, ready always to improvise, to use hints and implications . . . rather than actual representation. Let a player wearing a crown be a king: he will,

if he is an able player, convey all that is needed to an audience's mind; the exterior trappings of kingship are unnecessary . . .

Whilst the Company's founder regarded extreme simplicity and simplicity as desirable for The Theatre of Persons, the artistic possibilities of two hessian screens are so severely limited, that for some months the conception of an actual setting of screens remained embryonic. However, the Company's other visual asset was from the beginning made to serve artistic as well as practical ends. The two (soon increased to three) simple floodlights, while often essential in dim chancels and other ill-lit spots, were never used merely for illumination: by being fitted with coloured filters, they also gave character, atmosphere and unity to what was otherwise often an ugly and meaningless playing space.

In *Dr Faustus*, particularly, coloured light was used in this way. One light was placed on the floor at each side of the playing-space and directed across it obliquely. When one was given a straw and another a steel filter, the persons playing were at once given shape, highlight and shadow of contrasted colour.

When, for the scene of Faustus' conjuration of Mephistopheles, the straw-coloured filter was simply unplugged, the single steel light, hinting at moonlight, threw monstrous shadows behind the actors and gave a ghastly pallor to Brent's heavy make-up as Mephistopheles. Some readers, thinking of the effects they have seen developed in the great theatre of this country, may smile at the crudity of these lighting effects. Crude, I think, they were, as often as the make-ups, put on with difficulty in organ lofts and cleaner's cupboards (once we were offered a coal hole but declined). Though crude, the lighting was purposeful, immediate in its effect, and, by virtue of its very crudity, no end in itself but a direct contribution to the author's play.

Even in this elementary period three basic principles emerged which always remained at the root of all Adelphi lighting:

a) That the most important thing is to light an actor's face.
b) That the colour of a light is as important as its position.
c) That an even, overall lighting has no dramatic value.

Where the two, or three, home made floodlights were the only illumination, there was very little light available. However as the background to the actor was usually at best irrelevant, at worst distracting or dilapidated, the temptation to 'light the set' was absent. As has been acknowledged, the Adelphi Players often found themselves on the stages of Church Halls, Community Centres and the like, where the lighting provided was simply a row of naked bulbs above the proscenium, and sometimes a similar row as footlights. Therefore the Adelphi relied upon their own lighting, limited as it was, even when they found a stage well equipped with lighting, arranged in battens: horizontal rows of lights running across the top of the stage. In effect, the first four productions depended for their appearance upon: 1) That of each character; 2) Lighting; 3) Whatever the place of performance offered as playing-space and background. This last might be appropriate and impressive, like the magnificent heavy black curtains at Harrow School, or inappropriate and distracting like a dismal cinema at Nottingham. As the Company made, and later bought, additional lighting equipment, it was all in the form of floodlights and spotlights. When switchboards had to be designed and made, their fundamental principle was the independence of each light and the maximum of flexibility in control.

The production in which the characteristic Adelphi mode of screen setting was first used was *Easter*. Two more screens, identical with the original pair, were made for this, and for the first time it was possible to regard the screens as a 'setting' and not simply as 'masking'. This play, with its domestic interior, made new demands upon ingenuity. Two stools and chance were no longer adequate. Here then, was a definite kind of setting, not naturalistic, but able to suggest domestic interiors. In this production also, the producer – Martin Browne – had asked for a very simple 'fire' in the fourth wall to provide another focus for attention. This 'fourth wall' was not really liked by most of the Company. Whilst Martin Browne shared a great deal in common with the principles of the Adelphi, he did not, I think, share the strong urge to 'bust the proscenium' which was felt in the Company. Few things in the theatre emphasise the 'existence' of the 'fourth wall' and tend to keep alive in the mind of the audience the uncertainties it creates than does the fourth wall fireplace.

Following the schism of 1943, the Second Company, as has already been made clear, returned to the very basics in terms of staging. However, in productions such as *Squaring the Circle* and *Faust in Hell* they developed their use of lighting. To try to counteract some of the problems of light 'spillage' on constantly changing stages, the Company used an existing curtain set to continue the line of our screens upwards beyond the line of sight. In this way the combined screen and curtain became in effect a flat and the setting tended to look much more like a conventional 'box set', though lacking in height and in the usual paint.

Under Maurice Browne's first productions with the First Company some considerable strides were taken in the use of screen settings. In *Deirdre of the Sorrows*, for example, by setting the screens at right angles, to give an impression of massive solidity, and by using boldly coloured hangings, they contrived settings of a certain barbaric splendour yet without new elaboration and with no increase of banal naturalism.

Once the bare simplicities had been built upon, the danger was that naturalistic elements or features of lighting incompatible with screen setting might be introduced. When one looks at a photograph of the office scene in Ibsen's *An Enemy of the People* (October 1945) one sees what is, to all intents and purposes, a rather low box set lacking a ceiling. No attempt is made, at this stage, to continue the plane of the screens to above the sight-lines, but one feels that the setting, with its windows and door, and its straight un-screen-like walls, would have looked better if treated this way.

The First Company began to use the screens more and more in the manner of flats, the majority of which were 'booked': folded in pairs. Whilst the screens were not the painted flats of weekly repertory, they were painted a uniform grey. This was a practical measure to avoid the dirty impact upon unpainted hessian 'on the road'. A wealth of ingenuity, chiefly exercised by John Headley and Piers Plowman, had devised every conceivable sort of pelmet, arch, stove, fireplace, door, hanging etc so that such additions could be fitted to the 'screens' without their having to be damaged or pierced in any way.

Inevitably, after the Company had settled in Macclesfield as The Adelphi Guild Theatre, a new approach was needed to staging and setting. Three principle alterations were made in the settings during the first few months on the circuit system.

The first was the abandonment of the system of travelling a body of interchangeable units which could be employed in any new production. Each set was now regarded as a separate problem only related to others as far as economy dictated the re-use of older material. To implement this change, the Company engaged a full-time designer whose first task was to paint over the 'Adelphi grey'.

The second change was the gradual replacing of the existing seven-foot-six screens by ten-foot flats. Within the limited circuit of halls which the Company played, these were perfectly practicable and the change followed naturally enough.

The third major change, and for which I have to confess I was responsible, was that the Company acquired its own curtain set (at first of dyed hessian). The treatment of sets as composed of flats made it essential now that the top masking should always be complete. Setting now became a most laborious business, as the curtain set had to be shaped and flown before the setting proper could begin. What was intended to save labour seemed to create labour.

When fully developed, the Adelphi lighting – the origins of which are discussed earlier in this chapter – still based solely upon spotlights and floodlights, could produce almost any desired effect. There was sufficient equipment to hang a considerable bar of lights in the auditorium, have spotlights in perch positions (i.e. behind the proscenium) independent lighting for a 'Cyclorama' (Skycloth) and adequate lighting for all backings and the like that needed their own light sources. John Headley had, with Piers Plowman, designed and built the First Company's switchboard.

We have seen how at first, the demands of the production had to be very simple, and the plays were chosen, or written, accordingly. While it is true that, after the arrival of Maurice Browne, settings tended to become more decorative, their material pattern – their shape in space – was always functionally determined.

The Production

A good producer, in the Theatre of Persons, is a producer of actors. First and last a producer of Actors with the Adelphi Companies was anything but just the person who, as someone once expressed it to me, 'coaches the actors in their parts.' The producer as 'coach' was a conception utterly remote from the real situation in any phase of the Adelphi Companies. Yet, although in many ways there seems throughout to have been a consistency in attitude to the producer and in what he expected and what was expected of him, there was in fact great variety of method, partly arising from diversity of personalities, but also from differing needs and even, within limits, differing intentions. There is, I believe, a thread of consistency running through virtually all the productions, and while it is tempting to isolate certain phases as the 'best' or 'most typical', the picture will be truer, and more valuable, if shown in proportion and in its native untidiness. Inevitably, too, discussion of Production centres on the work of a few persons: there are two, Richard Ward and Maurice Browne, whose productions totally outweigh all the rest both in number and influence.

War conditions assured that at the beginning the producer would regard the producing of actors as his primary affair, there being little to distract him from this.

During the first two formative years, all the plays but one, *Easter,* were produced by Ward. As he was the Company's founder and Director, it was natural that the Company early got into the habit of regarding the producer as the ultimate authority on all matters relating to the show. That is not to say that actors and stage managers were not prepared to express disagreement with the producer.

Indeed, there were frequent discussions, arguments and even violent quarrels, but the final authority of the Producer/Director was unquestioned. This further indicates the delicate tensions in the Company between the extreme democracy practiced on the one hand, and the absolute authority granted to individuals in special spheres on the other. It was perhaps the strong sense of individual responsibility which made possible the strictness, even sometimes severity, of discipline in rehearsal.

This rehearsal discipline had special reactions in a Company of this type, too. Rehearsal is a communal activity. As there were no specialists, but every member an actor with other duties, people with costumes or properties to make might well have to work most, or occasionally all, of the night in order to complete their assignment, and still arrive fresh enough to rehearse next morning. To examine more specifically some rehearsals of the early Adelphi stages, I have selected *Holy Family* as particularly suitable for drawing attention to aspects of rehearsal peculiar to it. We start with the actual text. The cast had to give this unusually critical study before work could begin. The play, as we have seen, was for a homogeneous Chorus from which characters and groups crystallised from time to time, and while the producer had a fairly clear idea from the start as to how the principal emergent figures should be 'cast'.

The assignment of many lines, and the division of voices into semi-choruses and even smaller combinations could only be determined by experiments in their 'orchestration'. Further, as there could be no prompter and as changes in assigning lines might be made at any point in rehearsals, it was decided that everyone must know all of the play, which lasted just over an hour. Lines could then be allocated freely during later rehearsals and in the event of a memory lapse, instead of a prompt, another member of the Chorus would take up the words. As so much was chorally spoken everyone had to learn the play with the same emphases, inflections, tempi, pauses and the like.

For several days therefore, the cast sat in a circle and read and read and read, with frequent interruptions from Ward and from Phoebe Waterfield who, because of her experience in Martin Browne's production premiere of Eliot's *Murder in the Cathedral*, was given special responsibility for the choral speaking. The long period of reading, while particularly necessary in this play, rapidly became a normal feature of Adelphi production. Maurice Browne also emphasised its importance and would often devote one week of a three week rehearsal period to reading, before movement was begun. Consider the implications and effects of this approach. One is that the initial readings preceded the learning of the part. The choral speech created a special need for this in *Holy Family*, in that all had to learn with the same inflection. It is obviously best not to make a conscious effort to commit lines to memory until their basic meaning, some of the depth and implications, and the context in which they occur, have been fully studied and to a large extent assimilated in rehearsal.

Further, such learning will not be a mechanical grinding in of words, but the re-creation, below them, each time they are spoken, of a pattern of thought. The difficult places will be bridged by thought processes scored firmly in the mind as the lines themselves. Indeed, actors trained in these methods usually find the most important part of their private study in establishing these vital bridges in their minds. Again, the facility, valuable in a weekly repertory theatre, of being able, at first reading to present a superficially convincing interpretation, was regarded with deep suspicion in the Theatre of Persons. When the inner life is established in the actor, its theatrical expression can begin to grow. To do this organically and so deeply rooted that it grows afresh from its origin at every performance, it must be given time. Any outward acting of speech or movement which too rapidly acquires full shape and dimension, effective though it may be at a certain level, cannot be grown but must have been devised.

So Adelphi actors came to allow their performances to grow very slowly, and were not permitted to rush at facile interpretations. Just as the Chorus in *Holy Family* or *Destiny of Man* had to be human beings always, such slowly developing performances tended to become human before they became individualised.

Sometimes, in later phases, visiting producers found this characteristic distressing, the more so because some of the best actors were those whose performances developed very slowly and had often not reached maturity until they had been some time on the road.

The Adelphi gave absolute authority to the producer, who then did work most effectively when he used that authority as little as possible. At first, however, the original Adelphi Players was so inchoate, its personnel so inexperienced, that the producer-director had to give far more guidance, far more direct instruction, than he would have thought desirable had his cast been capable of assuming fuller responsibility for their individual interpretations. The person who clarified, developed and established most clearly a method of production within the Adelphi Companies was Maurice Browne. He made practical and theoretical contributions to Adelphi production which were assimilated into the common stock of knowledge and experience and became of real value to younger producers. In view of the deep impression that he made upon the Company's in productions, it is surprising to realise that he contributed little that was new. Yet his contribution was acceptable and effective simply because so much that he brought was in line with what already existed as Adelphi tradition. Also, coming at a time of divided loyalties, he, the powerful authoritarian, found eager followers. At a time of confusion, he, a precisan and codifier arranged muddled thoughts and feelings in some order (at the cost, unrealised by most of them, and perhaps by him, of oversimplification).

The discipline of rehearsals, and of all work connected with the preparation of shows, now became more severe.

Indeed, the degree of submission which Browne himself ultimately began to demand was such as to breed serious discontent. However that severity which, combined later with a desire to elaborate productions right up to the limits of practical possibility, served a valuable purpose during the period of 1943 to 1946 in maintaining, in spite of weariness and frequent adverse circumstances, a very high standard of work.

There was probably far less in common between the concepts of the Theatre of Persons, and Maurice Browne's concept of the theatre than there seemed to be then. However, the common ground lay in the most important region: the acting. Browne's production methods, at their best, were just what the young Company needed. Perhaps the subtlest duty of the producer with the Adelphi was to lead his actors to create a characterisation which is an integrated expression of the inner reality of the play as a whole.

The producer will tend, therefore to try to get the actor himself to decide to do what is necessary to the larger plan. Instead of giving commands he will ask questions. This rather Socratic method is slow as well as sure; it demands of the producer infinite patience and of the actor wholehearted cooperation. The method of scenic design that arises from this broader approach is diametrically opposed to that which one most frequently encounters. There, the design for a setting is brought forward, into which the producer fits his furniture and other material objects and his action. In relating these principles to the small stages for which Adelphi productions were designed, it was possible to define more precisely the minimum requirements to enable a play to be moved satisfactorily.

Where a very practical issue such as visibility was concerned, there was a factor caused by the fact that a great deal of the lighting used was cross lighting, which although effective, makes one actor cast his shadow upon another. Consequently, in the latter stages of production, if not the last stages of dress rehearsals, actors had to adapt themselves to a whole new set of technical problems.

During the final season of the Second Company, an experiment was devised in terms of production that arose out of practical necessity. As an experiment, however, it must be considered a failure, and any virtues the productions had were in spite of, rather than because of it. As there was little time and money was scarce, the experiment was to dispense with the role of a producer. An attempt was made, therefore, at production 'by members of the company in collaboration', as the programme stated of that period. I am glad that the attempt was made, though I doubt whether any of us involved would ever wish to repeat it.

A practice developed in the First Company for a time was for an inexperienced producer to get to work and carry the play to the point where it needed a more experienced hand to polish it, at which point Maurice Browne, with his personal assistant Molly Underwood, took over and remade the production where necessary.

5

PUBLIC RELATIONS AND THE PERSONS
OF THE THEATRE

We have examined the Adelphi Companies as organisms and organisations, fitness of their forms to their professions and purposes, the kinds of plays they presented, the manner in which they tried to present the means they used to these ends. In all, we have seen that the Companies were, imperfectly indeed, expressions of a kind of theatre I have called Theatre of Persons.

Every theatre, by its nature, is an experiment in public relations: indeed, the theatrical experience itself is a relationship between a company and its public. We ought to anticipate, on the basis of what we have already examined, that theatrical companies attempting to practice the principles of the Theatre of Persons will reveal their character very clearly in their public relations off-stage. Earlier in this book, I quoted from what Richard Ward had said after the Vicar where the first Church performance was given had referred to the original Adelphi Players, "as a body of people banded together in self-dedication", and had said that the Players had brought the spirit of St. Francis into the Church. In placing those sentiments into the context of the Company at that time, Ward had urged that they should not become "a burden upon our fellow's generosity". That is an odd phrase coming from the director of a Company of people who were working at all hours in difficult circumstances, for a pittance of £2 a week. However, something inherent in the implications of that phrase may offer a key to an understanding of Adelphi community relations, their aims, successes and failures.

For one thing, the phrase recognises the imperfection of the performances given and shows the realisation that the little the Company earned by its acting was really above its worth. The Players were always were very sensitive about their professional status. Performing in halls, schools, churches and other places usually used for amateur performances, they were likely to be taken for amateurs. This they were most anxious, naturally, to avoid. They felt profoundly that it was only because they staked their livelihoods on the acting that their existence as a Company was justified.

To understand this profound conviction, one must recall the emotional intensity of wartime, when no one – militarist or pacifist – felt that the country's life could be afforded any frills or decorations. Furthermore it could not be expected to support anyone not in some way wholeheartedly contributing to mitigate the universal suffering and danger. That anyone should have time and energy to indulge in what might be thought of as 'amateur theatricals' seemed inappropriate. Equally, the idea that young people, fit and in their prime, could so spend their lives would have been scandalous as much to the pacifists as to the militarists. By making the theatre their livelihood, and that livelihood austere, the Adelphi Players demonstrated their belief that they were making a genuine contribution to the lives of their fellow-countrymen in a time of conflict.

The Company were, therefore, received generally with sympathy and understanding, and their personal absorption in their work, their willingness to run risks and make sacrifices (at a time when greater risks and greater sacrifices were daily demanded of others) must have lent their performances some quality not unperceived by their audiences.

Technical weakness was not so much excused as, often, overlooked in face of evident integrity of purpose.

So, as Ward said, only the high aspirations of the Company could legitimately earn the Adelphi Players' bread and butter: as actors they were not yet worth a crust. Moreover, the **mere** performing of plays did not seem, against the background of the Battle of Britain, a justifiable occupation, whereas performing the kinds of plays, in the ways implied by Adelphi aspirations, did appear, even then, to justify itself. Whether, indeed, the little job we did, humbly and obscurely, was, in fact, adequate, seems impertinent to assert. But to us then, it seemed so. 'Official' society did not always push in our direction, and one Company member had to pay in terms of two months in prison for his freedom to work with us, instead of fulfilling certain other conditions of exemption from military service. On the whole, society's thrust was towards intensity, towards making one use oneself fully.

I recall a conversation in a commercial hotel in Bury St Edmunds. At table, the landlady began, in the manner of one who thinks she is about to uncover some unsavoury secret, to remark that what puzzled her was how it came about that so many men, young and apparently fit for military service, were permitted to remain in the Company and do this work. Our private lives, and at that time all the men were, for one reason or another (and in some way or another) conscientious objectors, were our own concern. While we all found the ideals of the Company to be in harmony with our objections to war, we found, both before and after it, that men who did not share our particular conviction had as real a place in the Theatre of Persons as we had.

If possible, we always avoided saying anything that would identify the Company as such with our private views. Indeed, this became a definite part of Company Policy. In the Minutes of a meeting on 26 June 1941 one finds:

> *Political Controversy*: Mr Ward renewed his request as director that members should avoid political arguments whenever possible and should particularly beware of branding the Company as a whole with their particular type of Pacifism, Anarchism, Socialism ... or any other 'ism'.[1]

Although in the first phase of the work many performances were given in Air Raid Shelters and similar places where there could only be a meagre collection, these had to be kept within limits, and the remaining performances were covered by guarantees. In other words, before the Company accepted any booking they had to have assurance that some person or organisation would guarantee them a minimum sum. This was usually five guineas for a full performance and three guineas for a shorter one such as *Abraham and Isaac*. Further, although they provided posters and handbills they had no organisation for distributing and bill-posting this material, and to have employed someone to have dealt with it, and to incur the full outlay involved would have been impossible. Therefore, not only was a guarantee required but also a Local Organiser. This Local Organiser, often a clergyman or Headmaster anxious to promote the good work of the Company, undertook a good deal. He arranged for the place of performance, assuming responsibility, of course, for any charges, if the box-office was insufficient; he raised the guarantee; he undertook all front-of-house arrangements, including tickets.

He received from the Company secretary a form to fill in giving many details which the Company needed to know, and a supply of posters and handbills which he must arrange to be displayed and distributed. In fact the Company were "subsidised" by the goodwill and hard work of a host of such Local Organisers who, if their work was unsuccessful had also to see that the guarantee was met, and so subsidised the Company financially as well. This special local contact, though obviously economically necessary and, to that extent, a liability, was not regarded simply as a device for overcoming difficulties, but also as a positive contribution to the Company-audience relationship.

---

1.   An essential, indeed, central aspect of Richard Ward's ideas and values that informed much of his own writing and work was his Pacifism. By the outbreak of World War Two in 1939, some progress had been achieved in terms of those many men who, like Ward, sought non-conscription to the Armed Forces on the basis of their principles and conscience. At the time of the First World War, many such men suffered tragically because of their beliefs. The Non-Conscription Fellowship, founded by ILP leader Fenner Brockway in 1914, campaigned for the Military Service Act of 1916 to ensure that conscientious objection was recognised as grounds for non-conscription. Nevertheless, this legislation was either ignored or unjustly disregarded by tribunals at that time. In fact, 73 conscientious objectors died as a result of the ill treatment they endured whilst in custody for their beliefs. Although public opinion towards conscientious objectors might generally be said to have improved between the wars, the decision not to take arms was one still needing courage and deeply-held principle. Ward, as an active member of the Peace Pledge Union, seemed to identify himself with the concept of the 'revolutionary pacifist' whom he describes in an article that he wrote for the PPU journal: *Peace News*: 'The conviction of the revolutionary pacifist is the necessity for the building of another social order: any step that he takes in that direction is a step in politics'. However, discretion clearly had to be the better part of valour in the circumstances under which the Adelphi Players lived and worked. An example of the potential adverse publicity and attention that a company such as the Adelphi Players might receive is seen in a front page headline from the *Coventry Evening Telegraph* of April 1942: "Adelphi Players now in Coventry, deny Pacifist Propaganda Allegation."

To begin with, the original Company took the road with an offer to the public: "The Players are willing to give performances at any time of day in any place, indoors or outdoors, where there is room for their audiences and themselves". Such an offer implies that the Players will not so much hope for audiences to come to them, as to go in search of the audience whether in "halls, theatres, churches, schools, clubs, air raid shelters, community centres, gardens, or private houses". Indeed, in its pattern of partnership between the full-time professional and the voluntary, part-time well-wisher and organiser, Adelphi policy had more in common with our traditional ideas about education than about Theatre. This partnership with local bodies and persons remained the basic policy throughout Adelphi history, departures from it being isolated exceptions only. Later, the actual relationships sometimes differed, and guarantees were not always asked, but even during the final phase of the Adelphi Guild Theatre at Macclesfield, the work was not carried on as by a wholly independent theatrical company. Rather, it was in close co-operation with, and with a vast amount of support from, the Macclesfield Playgoers Society, under its imaginative and energetic secretary, the Rev. Lismer Short.

Obviously such people are as important to the Theatre of Persons as the companies of players and without them this kind of set-up could not work.

The Players really entered into the lives of groups of people, whether the congregations of churches, the boarders and staff of public schools, the members of youth club or the troglodyte neighbourhoods of East End shelters. Again and again, minutes or accounts show real generosity on the side of the Company's "partners". We find such Minutes as: "Money from St. Alban the Martyr not yet to hand . . . Mr Housman's royalties were overdue. A letter was to be sent to him explaining that they could not be worked out until the gross takings of the Northampton week were known . . . However it was decided that Mr Housman be sent at once all royalties owing that we were in a position to calculate". For the majority of the Adelphi shows the Local Organisers undertook to provide some stage furniture, tables, chairs and so forth, to quite exacting specifications as to period and size. And remarkably well they managed, too, on the whole. The following anecdote illustrates, however, difficulties could arise.

When the Second Company were touring remote Women's Institutes in Scotland, they declared in advance that their only requirement was; 'one fifteen amp electric plug'. Arriving at one singularly out-of-the-way spot they were met by a young woman who, having welcomed them, added that she had had great difficulty in obtaining a fifteen amp plug for them. However, an expedition had eventually been made to a town some miles away which brought success and here it was: she held the plug out in her hand. There was no electricity in the village.

On the provincial tours which at first were incidental but which gradually grew to embrace the whole work, lodgings were a serious problem, for neither the individual nor the Company could afford to pay for them regularly.

Hospitality was therefore sought and was effectively another kind of subsidy without which the companies would not have survived.

Hospitality provided another field of Company – public contact. To live for months, or even for years on end in other people's houses, as a guest, is an experience quite as exhausting as interesting. A very early Minute says:

> "*Consideration for Hosts*: Mr Goding said in a very general terms that he felt that the company members ought to some extent to adapt their behaviour to avoid offending the susceptibilities of hosts and local organisers. He had felt on some occasions, that he did not specify, that the Company's behaviour might not have been wholly in harmony with the shibboleths of local organisers. Mr Palmer protested at the "mystery" of this suggestion and asked for specific instances. These were not forthcoming . . . Mr Ward, while declaring that up to the present he had not noticed anything to which Mr Gooding's suggestion might apply . . . added that actors, with their aura of Bohemia, might do well to study their behaviour . . . The prejudice that sometimes existed in people's minds against actors was easily broken down if actors showed themselves to be normal human beings".

But "normal human beings" are imperfect beings, and without doubt we were often seriously at fault in our behaviour. When the play was over, the make-up off, the properties packed up, we could not relax, but must be whisked off, with great good-will, of course, to various houses where, often alone, we had to sustain, if possible, entertaining conversation with our hosts . . . often having to exercise a good deal of diplomacy to avoid being drawn into political or religious controversy. This living on hospitality had other sides of course, and some lasting friendships arose between individual players and their hosts as a result of a night's hospitality. We became authorities on water closets and earth closets. I recall a WC in Surrey, on a ground floor, with a little notice in it: 'Please leave the window open so that the cat can get in.' At Morpeth, Ward found himself in a crazy lodging house kept by an old lady with dozens of dogs and cats (the dogs bit). There, when he pulled the chain, he was totally enveloped, out of the sky, by an ancient wool rug which had been put on the cistern against the frost, and, with the operation of the machinery, now descended upon him like a kind of booby-trap. Hospitality might be of the humblest, even the crudest kind. Two of us once spent a miserable and bitterly cold night, after no supper but half a mug of tepid cocoa, wooing sleep in a sort of barrack with only a torn blanket covering the door, which we shared with a number of young German refugees. Most of these had seen the inside of Nazi concentration camps and slept little better than we, several in their nightmares breaking out, from time to time, into semi-articulate German. On the other hand, one might find oneself in a wealthy and luxurious household where, in our simplicity, we might be out of our depth. Wilfred Harrison tells a story of his seeking to put out the light by means of what seemed to be a pull-cord. This however, came away in his hands and proved to be a pear-type bell-push. The mishap brought a foreign maid knocking at the door asking what was required.

Something must now be said about the kinds of bodies, voluntary and statutory, with which the Adelphi Players most frequently and fruitfully co-operated. As the initial emphasis was upon 'Religious and Educational' drama, much of the early work was done in co-operation with churches and schools. My own first Adelphi dressing room was an organ loft, shared with the rest of the Company. It was quite remarkable that the original Company played in co-operation with every degree of Protestantism and Catholicism from Westminster Cathedral Central Hall to the Quaker Meeting House in Northampton. The Church of England was its most frequent partner. In St Martin's in the Bull Ring, Birmingham, there was a magnificent structure of broad shallow steps, with wide platforms to two levels, from which Faustus was able to leap behind into a fiery 'hell'.

It was much the same with schools. A great variety wanted the Company's services, though naturally those with most independence were most easily able to engage them. Charterhouse, Harrow and Haileybury were among the Public Schools visited. Of Progressive schools there were, for example, Bedales and St Christopher's Letchworth. Nor were schools the only educational bodies involved. The Workers' Educational Association was a tower of strength, especially in the Potteries, at several stages in the Adelphi Players' history. As time went on Local Authorities began to assume more responsibility for arts and entertainment, especially in connection with the 'Holidays at Home' policy. Industry too, played its part, and on the first visit to the Potteries a performance was given in the Canteen at Spode-Copeland. Later, the development of ROF Hostels provided an entirely new type of contact with industrial audiences.[2] The Adelphi Players also found channels for work through many individual societies and bodies.

The Friends Ambulance Unit, for instance, promoted a performance at its Birmingham headquarters.[3] The Bank Clearing House, evacuated to Trentham Gardens, Stoke-on-Trent, had its own theatre, The Siren Theatre, which welcomed the Company. However, the finest amity and co-operation was at Ilkley, where the Ilkley Players not only arranged for the Adelphi to perform in their excellent little theatre, the Ilkley Playhouse, but soon after made a generous offer which resulted in the Ilkley Playhouse becoming the Adelphi headquarters, used for rehearsals and opening performances.

The keynote of the initial policy undoubtedly was that of personal service: the Company existed for the service of others, the play was produced and performed in the service of others. In that service one obviously chose the

---

2.   Royal Ordnance Factories.
3.   FAU were ambulance units instigated by the Religious Society of Friends (Quakers) at the time of the First World War. Many conscientious objectors found the opportunity for service and War Work by working as volunteers on the FAU's. They were in particular and devastating demand during the Blitz.

play one felt to be of greatest service to one's fellows, and one sought to perform it as well as possible for the sake of others.

It seems now as if that ideal of service was gradually lost sight of in the search for the elusive "standards" which we have already discussed fairly fully. In some strange way, the original integrated ideal became lost. Even the terms of difference between those forming the First and those forming the Second Company in 1943, show that the dichotomy between artistic standards and social service was in existence. In the First Company particularly a tendency developed to establish absolute artistic standards at which one aimed, adapting all else in policy to that aim – kind of hall played in, kind of audience catered for, kind of tour undertaken until eventually the whole pattern of life was radically changed, partly indeed because the number of married people who wanted some stability of life had increased, but largely because it felt that some sort of "regional" system would enable the "standard" to be raised higher than it could be on "wild-cat touring".

From whatever perspective one approaches the work of the Adelphi Players one returns to the same central issue in the end: that their original strength lay simply in the centrality of the person. This applied whether that person was actor, member of audience, or characters within the play. The experiment developed and was fruitful while art and life went hand in hand, when the Theatre of Persons was not an ideal for the stage, but a way of life actually practised by the actors, on stage and off it: when serving the persons in the audience was as important as the art on the stage, and when the art on the stage was as important as the service to others, when it, in fact, was that service and existed for others: and not for the sake of some purely artistic ideal, however high.

The Persons of the Theatre

Actors in the Theatre of Persons are experimentalists and spiritual athletes, and they run the risk of all experimentalists and athletes. One way of counteracting that risk is not to work in this way for too long at one time. The need in the early days of the Adelphi for every person to carry several responsibilities was a necessity with great virtue, and wise people within the Theatre of Persons have always seen to it that, as the Quakers put it, the actor's "work has such a background as to make attainable a true balance of life".

The stage-management, porterage, van and bus-driving, route-planning, transport arrangements, carpentry and sewing – all undertaken by people who were also actors and actresses helped to preserve that balance, and the increasing specialisation between 1947 and 1949 in Macclesfield, while it may have brought about technical improvements, did much to destroy the personal character of the theatre. In thus declaring in favour of the whole person rather than the specialist, the Theatre of Persons proclaims itself heretical in twentieth-century society. The Theatre of Persons says that the persons are more important than the theatre. It likes a leading actor who can work a switchboard or dismantle an internal combustion engine. Clearly, the people likely to be attracted into the Theatre of Persons were not, on the whole, what were usually called 'theatre people'. Ward himself had for many years worked outside the theatre as an author, pamphleteer, speaker and journalist.

Phoebe Waterfield and Greta Newell alone were trained professional actresses. Later Company members included Wilfred Harrison who had a degree in Science, John Crockett was a remarkably fine painter whilst Bernard Rumball had acted in Nugent Monck's Maddermarket Theatre in Norwich.[4] Piers Plowman had given up reading Physics at Oxford because he felt that this subject could not be used creatively in wartime. Given agricultural work by a Tribunal, he had worked, after his father's death, at The Oaks, but in 1942 broke his condition of exemption in order to join the Company. For this, he later suffered two months in Wormwood Scrubs as his penalty. Another person who should be remembered was Ward's wife Jenny, who in the early days, when she wasn't driving an ambulance in the Blitz, was designing or sewing costumes. Molly Sole was also another vital and indispensable person, whose contribution to the Adelphi work from beginning to end was perhaps greater than that of any other single person. At first she arranged all the bookings, she kept records, minutes, press-cuttings, photographs, diaries. She linked the First and Second Companies, she mediated between the Companies and CEMA, she dealt with government departments, smoothed over difficulties, promoted development. During the touring phases no sight was more welcome than Molly arriving on a visit on 'Poppy' – her Frances-Barnett – or later, in her Austin Seven: 'Matilda'. Without the records kept by her, this book could not have been written. There were, of course, many other people who worked in or with the Adelphi who soon moved away in other directions. Of those who were deeply involved over a long period only a very few have pursued their career into the wider world of established theatre. The lack of specialisation within the Adelphi framework did produce people who were at some disadvantage outside that framework.

However, the primary reason for many moving out of the theatre was simply and truly that those people were just not interested in, or attracted by, any theatre except the Theatre of Persons. They were, frankly, more interested in humanity than in the theatre and if they could not work in the

---

4.   A theatre based in Norwich and founded by Nugent Monck (1877–1958) who was an English actor and director. Built inside a dilapidated hall in Norwich 1921, Monck intended to try and re-create the staging conditions of the Elizabethan Playhouse. Monck was an ardent disciple of William Poel (1852–1934) who founded the English Stage Society in 1894 and was highly instrumental in the revitalised approach to the staging of and production of Shakespeare in the first half of the twentieth century. Poel's ideas and experiments have had a substantial influence on later developments, and Ward's own ideas regarding the minimalist production of Shakespeare owes much to Poel's thinking.

kind of theatre that interested them, preferred to find channels for expressing their human interests elsewhere.

There is a good reason for concluding this book about the Adelphi Players with a chapter on Persons of the Theatres. It is with the persons that this theatrical 'experiment' began, and with them that it ended. Max Plowman was a significant person in the origins of the Adelphi and I would like to end with a quotation from his book *War and the Creative Impulse*:

> "What a work is man" and what can compare for beauty with a man or woman who is manifestly a complete human personality. Such an one radiates benificence ... 'He appears to be without need, yet friendship is his element and the smallest human emotion finds him vibrant. He grips the earth with his feet: his eyes are level with his fellows'; his mind can soar into infinity ... In him the past and future meet, and therefore he is without hankerings for either ... Out of his riches and not because of his poverty, he is a democrat.

> Why is this glorious creature to be found
> One only in ten thousand? What one is,
> Why may not millions be? What bars are thrown
> By Nature in the way of such a hope?

EPILOGUE

A RETROSPECT

When, a few years ago, I decided that my almost contemporary account of the work of the Adelphi Companies was now, despite its naivity and lack of perspective, worth publishing as a primary source for study of some aspects of theatre history I realised that I ought not to edit it myself, nor did I wish to.

It is always an error for an elderly author to tinker with the spontaneous outpourings of his youth. Yet edited it must be, for it was too verbose and too often expatiated on side-issues of doubtful relevance. Peter Billingham, in editing the text, has removed some dross and highlighted the ideological essentials of how we were motivated and how our aims were embodied in practice. One qualification to write on the subject was uniquely mine, for I was the only person (not excepting Richard Ward himself) who had worked in all the Adelphi Companies, including the Adelphi Guild Theatre.

From the perspectiver of the new millenium I become keenly aware that the work of the Adelphi Players belongs to, and is firmly rooted in the mid-twentieth century, the period of the Second World War and its immediate aftermath. At that time our aims and ideals appeared to us to have universal significance. In some ways, indeed, they had, but in their particular forms and expression they were products of their period. And so were we. Nearly all of us were in our twenties and had grown up in the world between the wars. Although Richard Ward was a little older (he was born in 1910) he had been educated and had matured in that period. He had travelled abroad as an actor, had written several successful novels, and had worked in the Bloomsbury Office of the Peace Pledge Union when we were still school-children or students. He was thus near enough to us to be one of us, while also able to exercise leadership and authority.

Although no saint, Richard possessed what it has become fashionable to call charisma. He could be cruel, especially to the women in his life, but was also capable of intense love and friendship in his relations with both men and women. Looking back I realise that Richard was what we should now call my guru.

His portrait, by John Crockett, shows clear blue eyes that are keen but questioning, and a mouth with tightly closed lips whose corners are turned down with a hint of mercilessness. His long-fingered sensitively expressive hands speak the actor, while one finger of his left hand keeping his place in a book suggests impatience to be done with the portrait so that he can resume his reading.

Not only were we as persons the product of our adolescence, but so also was our concept of theatre. Brecht was virtually unknown: Eric Bentley translated *Mother Courage* (written in 1939) in 1941, the year the Adelphi Players were founded. Stanislavsky was still felt to be the prophet of modern theatre. In 1939 I had been told to study *An Actor Prepares* as part of my post-graduate course for a Teacher's Diploma. The rehearsal methods encouraged in the Adelphi companies had a great deal in common with those of Stanislavsky – though we never adopted the kinds of exercises used by Lee Strasberg in the name of Stanislavsky from 1948 onwards at the New York Actors' Studio. Indeed, I think we would have found some of these developments merely silly. Nevertheless we were, I believe, justified in regarding ourselves as ahead of our times, however crude the results of our experiments might be. When we first came into being orthodox theatre was still dominated by the front curtain (tabs) and the box set. The circumstances of our performances normally precluded both these and we made a virtue of necessity, adopting as our own the phrase "Proscenium Busting", coined first by Sybil Thorndike.

We were not dogmatic about this and when we met a stage with tabs we used them. Certainly none of us could have foreseen a time when a front curtain would provide welcome relief from looking at unlit sets on the bare stage while sitting in the auditorium waiting for "Curtain Up"(!). Of course in the broader, philosophic sense of communicating directly with the audience we did always aim at breaking the barrier which the proscenium arch symbolises.

In our use of screens we were by no means as deeply influenced by Edward Gordon Craig as we would have liked to believe, and when the need arose to represent, for example, a window, we used a pelmet and gauze curtain to this end. We did this first as early as February 1942 in Strindberg's *Easter* where the threatening shadow of the dreaded creditor Lindkvist is thrown on the curtains by the street lamp. In this production, too, we even suggested the Fourth Wall by using a low fireplace into which the birch rod is thrown at the end. Admittedly this production was directed by E. Martin Browne who probably had less enthusiasm than we had for screen settings.

But realism was still customary in British theatre and by the time the Adelphi Guild Theatre was established we were building convincingly three-dimensional naturalistic settings for all productions, and when I, as designer, offered drawings of a highly stylised setting for J. B. Priestley's *Eden End*, Jack Brent as Director rejected it out of hand. Looking back, I am sure he was right, but it hurt at the time.

In one respect (one that was essential to the Theatre of Persons) we were deeply realistic: namely in our treatment of the inner life, the psychology of characters. Every movement, gesture, inflection had to be justified by the inner psychological line – what today we call the sub-text. In 1948 we did

Denis Johnston's *The Moon in the Yellow River*. It was to be directed by Ted Willis, but he had to withdraw at the last moment, even after he had approved the design of the set, so I had to take over. At one point in rehearsal Bettina Stern, as Agnes, was having difficulty with part of a speech. I, ever impatient, said we should press on and return to the problem passage later. But Bettina would have none of this. She could not speak the subsequent speeches rightly if the inner thread of the character's thoughts and feelings had been broken. Some might say this was unprofessional, but in fact it was the measure of the depth of her commitment to our kind of professionalism.

From the viewpoint of half a century later it is clear that the most important single factor determining the nature and indeed the very existence of the Adelphi Companies was the Second World War and its aftermath. Had there been no war, no threat of the bombing of London, no closure of theatres, no flight from the capital, the Adelphi Players would not have been founded. Had there been no war there would have been no body of conscientious objectors, most of them untrained in theatre, but talented and eager to serve the community in their own way. Had there been no war there would have been no demand for a small group of actors ready to perform 'wherever there was room for themselves and an audience', be it a cellar at Smithfield Market or a village hall in the Highlands. The war familiarised everyone with the concept of 'billeting', whether of the Armed Forces or of evacuees.

Therefore the requirement that the actors, once away from London, must be given hospitality was seen as quite normal. The blackout and many limitations on travelling created new audiences, both in air-raid shelters and in remote areas. Above all, perhaps it was the psychology of wartime, and of the years of austerity that immediately followed it, that embraced soldiers and conscientious objectors alike, and made discomfort and generosity both seem inevitable. It is true that some civilians only accepted us because they did not know specifically that we were conscientious objectors and once, after Piers Plowman and I, having been plied by our host, the local doctor, with more whiskey than we were accustomed to, had let out that we were conscientious objectors, the company was more or less drummed out of the village the next morning. This was exceptional, however, and normally we were wholly accepted in the communities we visited, sharing their lives, even to the occasional air-raid. It was the war which made acceptable to ordinary people ("The Man on the Clapham Bus") our repertoire, fundamentally serious, educational and even religious. Our plays were wanted in halls, churches, parks, and even Royal Ordnance Factory Hostels. Wherever we went we found ourselves at home.

We were an extraordinarily closely knit group. At a memorial Service in 1997 for Seamus Stewart, a Quaker, Adelphi Players from all periods, even from 1941, were present! It was appropriate that the Memorial Service was ecumenical, conducted by priests and laity of every denomination in Chipping Campden from Catholic to Quaker, for as a group we had always been happy to mix with all sorts and conditions of people.

Christmas Day 1941 is never to be forgotten and has always seemed to me to epitomise our life and work. About mid-day we arrived with our very minimal equipment at the United Services Club, almost in the shadow of Big Ben. We were made welcome and I recall that we had the use of the bar. Our performance was of Christopher Marlowe's *Tragical History of Doctor Faustus*. In Richard Ward's brilliantly-cut version our production concentrated on the central theme of Modern Man who sells his soul for knowledge and power:

> O, what a world of profit and delight,
> Of power, of honour, of omnipotence,
> Is promised to the studious artisan!
> All things that move between the quiet poles
> Shall be at my command

In that place and at that time, the 'hellish fall' of Faustus, as a warning to mankind not

> To practise more than heavenly power permits

seemed to us to speak to the condition of a world at war.

Our performance, as conscientious objectors, of Marlowe's tragedy in what we felt to be the very heart of militarism, would alone have been a noteworthy experience. But there was more to come. In the evening we went to Bethnal Green, where a huge tube-station, not yet in service for its proper function, acted as one of London's largest Air Raid Shelters. Such shelters were now the nightly home of many who did not wait for an air raid before seeking their protection.

So we descended, in company with many others, the long, steep, straight flight of stairs leading to the station's great steel doors. We did not know, and could not foresee, that later in the war a panic rush down these very stairs when the doors below were closed and locked, would lead to many fearful deaths in the crush at the bottom.

To our surprise we found that, unlike some shelters in which we had performed, this had been fully adapted for its purpose. Where the station was widest much of its width had been taken up by an auditorium and a stage with tabs and battens of lights. Here our play was Richard Ward's *Holy Family*, in its first version – the refreshingly heretical one – for which we wore modern dress, with no settings or properties save a three-legged stool for the pregnant Mary. It was with a nation of troglodytes that we identified in our opening Chorus:

> We live, if we do live at all, in a darkness of death.
> Death is our being. Death is the life of our age.

Perhaps we brought some cheer to our audience at the conclusion, when we declared that:

> I see beyond death to the place of eternal change
> Where all things revolve on themselves and end is beginning
> And hope is renewed in despair.

No doubt we were naive. It was only 1941. The worst of the war and the Holocaust were still to come, but it was Christmas Day and we had taken Marlowe's grim warning to the Forces and Richard Ward's vision of hope even in despair to the civilians of the underground. For me at least Christmas Day 1941, because of the Adelphi Players, remains the most memorable of my whole life.

APPENDIX A

A Complete List of Plays in Repertoire 1941–1951

1941   *Holy Family*   R. H. Ward
           The Little Plays of St Francis   Laurence Housman
           Dr Faustus   Christopher Marlowe
           Abraham and Isaac   Laurence Housman
           The Actors are at Hand   R. H. Ward

1942   *Don Juan*   James Elroy Flecker
           Easter   August Strindberg
           The Three Maries   Cornish Mystery Play
           Comus   John Milton

1943   *Bernice*   Susan Glaspell
           Mrs Henley   R. H. Ward
           The Duchess of Malfi   John Webster
           Ghosts   Henrik Ibsen
           The Heroic Legend of Robin Hood   R. H. Ward
           The Sulky Fire   Jean-Jacques Bernard

1944   *The Bachelor*   Ivan Turgenev
           Deirdre of the Sorrows   J. M. Synge

1945   *Twelfth Night*   William Shakespeare
           Shadow and Substance   Paul Vincent Carroll
           An Enemy of the People   Henrik Ibsen

1946   *Mr Bolfry*   James Bridie
           Arms and the Man   Bernard Shaw
           The Unknown Warrior   Paul Raynal

1947   *I Have Been Here Before*   J. B. Priestley
           The Duke in Darkness   Patrick Hamilton
           The Moon in the Yellow River   Denis Johnston
           Thunder Rock   Robert Ardrey
           It Depends What You Mean   James Bridie
           Hedda Gabler   Henrik Ibsen
           Toad of Toad Hall   A. A. Milne

1948   *Eden End*   J. B. Priestley
        She Stoops to Conquer   Oliver Goldsmith
        The Wise Have Not Spoken   Paul Vincent Carroll
        An Inspector Calls   J. B. Priestley
        The Whole World Over   Konstantin Simonov /
                                                             Thelma Schnee
        The Dragon   Lady Gregory

1949   *Simpleton of the Unexpected Isles*   Bernard Shaw
        The Merchant of Venice   William Shakespeare
        Tobias and the Angel   James Bridie

1950   *The Hasty Heart*   John Patrick
        Sheppey   Somerset Maugham
        Alice in Wonderland   Lewis Carroll
        Dandy Dick   Arthur Wing Pinero
        Land of the Living   Leonard Irwin
        Macbeth   William Shakespeare

1951   *The Bubble*   Leonard Irwin
        Mr Gillie   James Bridie
        The Rose and the Ring   W. M. Thackeray
        The Prince of Darkness is a Gentleman Cecil Davies
        Prophesy to the Wind   Norman Nicholson

APPENDIX B

Music Composed by Phoebe Waterfield
for the Adelphi Players production of
The Ordinalia – The Three Maries

This particular Mystery Play may well have originated from one of the earliest surviving examples of Liturgical Drama. Originating in the trope or sung/ chanted text – for the Easter Liturgy, "Quem quaeritis" (meaning "Whom seek ye?") tells the story of the Three Maries coming upon the Angel at the empty tomb of Christ. Elliott Martin Browne, in collaboration with writers like Eliot and Duncan, played a principal role on the revival and production of mediaeval Mystery and Morality Plays. Inevitably, this led to research and debate concerning the precise nature and use of music within performance. Interestingly, in the light of the Adelphi experience with *The Ordinalia* at Birmingham, a British authority on liturgical drama, Dr W. L. Smoldon, argued for his belief that the only accompaniment provided for these early dramas was organ and chime-bells. His view was that these would have been used in a simple, minimalist fashion, similar to the means chosen by the Adelphis.

P. Billingham

INDEX

Other titles in the Contemporary Theatre Studies series:

Other titles in the Contemporary Theatre Studies series:

This book is part of a series. The publisher will accept continuation orders which may be cancelled at any time and which provide for automatic billing and shipping of each title in the series upon publication. Please write for details.